GHOSTS OF TOM JOAD

PETER VAN BUREN

LUMINIS BOOKS

Published by Luminis Books
1950 East Greyhound Pass, #18, PMB 280,
Carmel, Indiana, 46033, U.S.A.
Copyright © Peter Van Buren, 2014

Cover design for *Ghosts of Tom Joad* by Rachel Marks. Cover image courtesy
Shutterstock.

Hardcover ISBN: 978-1-935462-90-3
Paperback ISBN: 978-1-935462-91-0

Printed in the United States of America

10 9 8 7 6 5 4 3 2 1

LUMINIS BOOKS

Meaningful Books That Entertain

Praise for *Ghosts of Tom Joad:*

"Politicians come and go, but the critical issues tearing at our society do not. In his new book *Ghosts of Tom Joad,* Van Buren turns to the larger themes of social justice and equality, and asks uncomfortable questions about where we are headed. He is no stranger to speaking truth to power, and the critical importance of doing that in a democracy cannot be overestimated. Standing up and saying 'This is wrong' is the basis of a free society. The act of doing so must be often practiced, and regularly tested."

—Daniel Ellsberg, whistleblower, *The Pentagon Papers*

"A lyrical, and deeply reported look at America's decline from the bottom up. Though a work of fiction, *Ghosts of Tom Joad* is—sadly, and importantly—based on absolute fact. Buy it, read it, think about it."

—Janet Reitman, contributing editor, *Rolling Stone*, author of *Inside Scientology: the Story of America's Most Secretive Religion*

"At the State Department Peter Van Buren was a pioneer blowing the whistle in defense of human rights by challenging torture. In this novel, he blows the whistle in defense of America's roots by challenging the dehumanizing consequences when big business abandoned the Rust Belt in Ohio. This tale of a mythical Earl's relentless quest for an American dream that has become a mirage is worthy of the voices that inspired it, from Woody Guthrie to John Steinbeck to Bruce Springsteen."

—Tom Devine, Legal Director, Government Accountability Project

"Van Buren is passionate about the truth, and his new book *Ghosts of Tom Joad* is a masterpiece, a must-read about the decline of our economy and social structure, an inspirational story showing how one man and one nation can claw its way back to greatness."

—Kathryn Milofsky, Producer Reporter ITV (UK) / Executive Producer of "The Brian Oxman Show" (US)

"A twenty-first century *Grapes of Wrath,* this memorable volume documents in a concrete, personal, often moving way the despair among many in America today due to economic and family hardships. In the words of its fictional but all too real narrator—Earl, from a rust-belt small Ohio town, unable get a permanent job or start a family —'they took away the factory, but left the people; this ain't a story, it's an autopsy.'"

—John H. Brown, Adjunct Professor of Liberal Studies, Georgetown University

"In Peter Van Buren's *Ghosts of Tom Joad,* things do not always look better in the morning. In this autopsy of the new depression, you turn a page and keep reading, hoping the story's left-behind people catch up . . . because one way or another, they're us."

—Diplopundit

"In *Ghosts of Tom Joad,* Peter Van Buren invokes his powerful story-telling gifts to portray a job-starved Ohio community. This gripping, contemporary novel in the tradition of *The Grapes of Wrath* is more real than real—and a worthy successor to Van Buren's reporting about Iraq in his courageous *We Meant Well.*"

—Andrew Kreig, Director, Justice Integrity Project

"*Ghosts of Tom Joad* is a powerful and provocative tale of the working poor. Although the story is fiction, the themes are anything but. In a lively yet serious manner, Peter Van Buren tackles one of the most important issues of our day—how can a free society deal with the costs associated with creative destruction? *Ghosts of Tom Joad* is required reading for all concerned with the future of our country."

—Christopher J. Coyne, F.A. Harper Professor of Economics, George Mason University

"*Ghosts of Tom Joad* takes a hard, honest look at where millions of Americans are today: living a marginal existence, a no-exit life of grinding poverty. What Peter Van Buren is able to show through his gritty, close-to-the-ground prose, is how capitalism destroys the human spirit, leaving its victims devoid of any purpose in life. Those of us in our sixties and seventies are completely bewildered at where the America of our youth—a very different sort of place from today—went. The answer is contained in the pages of this book: the values of 'the market' finally swamped everything else, destroyed any values except those of rapaciousness and self-interest. 'I think God owes us an apology,' says the central character of this novel. No, I'd reply; but America certainly does."

—Morris Berman, historian and author of *The Twilight of American Culture, Dark Ages America: The Final Phase of Empire* and *Why America Failed: The Roots of Imperial Decline*

"I can't tell you what an impact this book had on me. The writing is beautiful, but the story is brutal. I grew up in and around these places, and to say it is grim is an understatement. *Ghosts* captures everything—the human complexity and the profound cultural/economic damages. The story stuck with me long after I stopped reading."

"I grew up and later worked in a 'Reeve, Ohio.' While experiencing a visceral recognition, Van Buren's intimate portrait of this dying town made me feel like a stranger peeking in on places many Americans have no idea exist. I will never again drive by the old manufacturing towns of my youth without wondering about the shadows within, as drawn so mesmerizingly in Van Buren's relentlessly vivid portrayal. As Steinbeck's *Grapes of Wrath* made a place for the Dust Bowl in our literary canon, *Ghosts* aims to do the same for the devastating industrial decline of the late-American 20th century."

—Kelley Vlahos, *The American Conservative*

"Bottom line: It's accessible and compelling, a mix of *Canterbury Tales* meets *Grapes of Wrath* meets *American Beauty*."

—Charlie Sherpa, military blogger, *Red Bull Rising*

"Have and have-nots have always existed. *Ghosts of Tom Joad* brings this conflict so often touched upon in literature into a modern day, down-turned economy. Riveted with a bit of nostalgia for the rosier '70s and '80s, the story manages to find humor in an otherwise dismal life. When you choose to ride this bus with Earl, you'll find yourself reminiscing with him, rooting for him, and yearning for the release he strives to find."

—Lisa Ehrle, Teacher-Librarian, Aurora, Colorado.

"Haunting and a kick in the gut, Peter Van Buren's first novel, *Ghosts of Tom Joad*, lays bare the brutal and very personal reality of America's Great Recession. In his first book, *We Meant Well*, Peter blew the whistle on the catastrophic effects of American policy in Iraq; now Peter turns his necessary and just attention on the effects of American policy at home. Want to understand the true and honest nature of our modern society and the American way of life? Then read *Ghosts of Tom Joad*."

—Matthew Hoh, Peace and Veterans advocate, former Marine

"Peter Van Buren has an amazing ability to draw the reader into his stories. That the author of the definitive work on the debacle of our post-war reconstruction of Iraq has now set his sights on the debacle of our post-industrial America makes perfect sense. Many of the actors are the same, with the same intent."

—Daniel McAdams, Ron Paul Institute

"Like his heroes in Steinbeck and Agee before him, the author takes us on an unflinching tour of America's 'broken places,' yet true to his predecessors Van Buren never loses sight of his rough characters' resilient humanity, their deeply held yearning for the grounding connection of family and community, their stubborn hope for a better life. An urgent, important story, and an incredibly necessary book."

—James Spione, Academy-Award nominated documentarian, *Incident in Baghdad* and *Silenced*

For Woody—this book kills fascists.

Prologue

LET THE YOUNG men in other small Ohio towns dream of bright lights. In Reeve, Ohio we knew growing up we were going to work in that factory. We said, "Graduate today, factory tomorrow." Life was rich, fat, happy enough. But we thought that factory in Reeve was drawn in ink, when it was really watercolor. After she closed on us, I was a telemarketer. A tire salesman, one McJob after another. Christmas help. The development that had been planned for Reeve, the one that was gonna bring in big retail stores and jobs for everyone, fizzled on some complicated six-way derivative financing deal, and so, long after they tore down the factory, the land stayed vacant. There were pieces of machinery from the factory left on the ground, too unimportant to sell off, too heavy to move, too bulky to bury, left scattered like clues from a lost civilization, droppings of our failure. Might as well been the bones of the men who worked there. I think God owes us an apology.

I climbed out of the foxhole to see almost every one of them running in circles, throwing snowballs at each other and shouting, laughing and throwing some more snowballs. Boredom and young boys do not mix well and after what seemed like forever doing nothing, we had found something. I packed a tight one, pulling off my gloves so as to let my hands melt the snow enough to form an ice ball. With some element of a practiced eye, I hurled that snowball as hard as I could at some boy about twenty yards away, smacking him straight on his nose. He looked over at me more surprised than anything and when I saw him laugh, I laughed too and went over to make sure there were no hard feelings. His nose was bloodied all right, as I had something of an arm back then, with the red blood dripping on that white snow. As he laughed, his head moved, flinging the drops of blood in a wider circle around us both. It was kinda pretty, the red and the white, the drops giving off a tiny bit of steam and melting just a tiny bit into the crust of the snow.

The CEO of Wal-Mart's hourly wage works out to $8,701. An entry-level Wal-Mart clerk in Arkansas makes six bucks an hour, below minimum wage, because she's a trainee under local law.

In a decent world that would have been the end of that day. I would have walked home, had dinner, maybe asked my own father about what had happened. Going to bed and waking up the next morning usually solved problems in the small town of Reeve, Ohio, as many times the smell of a new day absorbed what had passed the night before.

In the last thirty years, the share of national income of the top one percent of Americans doubled. For most of the remaining 99 percent of households, the share went down.

But I was not there, I was as far away from there as it was possible to be, and so I heeded the Sergeant and ran to my hole. Whatever that man knew about whores and cursing, he did know equally about the real side of war that had just been visited on me, and so I ran to my hole and, following his shouts, prepared and aimed my rifle forward, expecting the North Koreans or maybe Satan himself to emerge from those woods.

At the time of the fall of Rome only two thousand people owned all of the land between the Rhine and the Euphrates rivers. In 2014, 85 people own half of the world's wealth.

There is nothing in the world that sounds like a mortar. We did not know whether it was the noise we made, the movement we made on Hill 124, or simply one of those coincidences that caused mortar shells to fall on us twenty or so boys making snow angels. We did not know if the mortar shells were fired by our men, North Korean men, or spit out by an angry God, but they did fall on us. The snow did its job, deadening the sound of the explosions, catching some of the shrapnel, which, white-hot, made some tiny puffs of steam as it melted through the snow crust, and then absorbing the fluid of several boys, one from Indiana recently suffering from a bloody nose. I was fine, not hurt, just watching the impressions of snow angels fill with blood around me as Hill 124 tried to kill us.

(Me now, inhaling, deep breath. Remembering's the only thing I got left. Click. BANG. An alarm clock goin' off.)

A Snowball's Chance in Hell

THE LONGEST DAY of my life started when I accidentally shot myself. Went downhill from there, as you'll soon see.

Don't feel bad for me, though I probably have a snowball's chance in hell. And that's sort of okay, I guess. I'm Earl, and I've been riding a bus around my hometown of Reeve, Ohio. My nerves was fragile as the sound of boots on cold gravel and, to be fair, at some point I was just seein' unhealthy shadows, like standing up too quickly, head tingly, and was resigned to riding this bus all day and night. The road to Hell now has bus service. Squeal, whoosh, doors open with a puff of inside-outside air changing, people get on and off, and I sat here. It was something to do, a way to pass the time since I couldn't find steady work. Safe, steady in its own way, like old black and white shows on the TV. It's not a bad life, or it wasn't, until today.

See, at one point there were patterns that made simple sense as the Driver followed the same route around town. The doors would slap open and closed, reminding me how when I was a baby, my mom, I guess, would push me on the swings sayin' "Back and a-wwwway, back and a-wwwway" as I swung. We weren't that small of an Ohio town anymore that everyone knew where to go, but we weren't big enough that you were afraid to talk to a stranger on the bus.

And that's part of what made this day on the bus different, the strangers. For the most part, I knew them only as Fat Guy with Laptop, in his shirt like a sausage casing, or Woman with Noisy Child, or Old Man with a face like you'd see in a commercial for gas bloat medicine. A lot of times too, I saw a young Korean boy in the back of the bus, shadowy places under his eyes that one, kinda scary if a kid could be scary. Never said anything, probably didn't speak English, but a lot of them had moved to town. Then, somehow, the people on the bus became more familiar—really familiar—until even I had to recognize that I knew almost all of them.

Or had known them—most of the folks who get on the bus with me have been long missing from my life of fifty-two years. Now they were coming and going, even talking to me, just as if it was no big deal that they were like ghosts. It was like having a super power. I was the Hulk of mental illness. It's one thing to hear voices in your head telling you to love some famous actress or smear purple paint on your chest, but it's another to run into both your mom and your old girlfriends in living color on a bus. But it seems everybody you run across in life you drag forward. You can't help that. They're all on the bus with you.

It is quiet now, and we're about to stop for someone. This happens all the time. I'm envious that they get to climb on and off, when all I really would like is to finish this ride. That's the last big question I got to answer: how to get off this bus.

My best friend from high school, Muley, got on and sat down behind me. His real name was Thomas, but only his mom and Mrs. Garrity the English teacher who said she believed in him called him that. Most of us called him Muley, an unfortunate leftover from an unfortunate puberty thing in sixth grade. In towns like this we don't forget, but we do compensate. Just like my friend Rich, who moved in to Reeve from Gibbsville, and who twelve years later was still known as the new kid, and always will be.

The summer of 1977 was the hottest one any of us not yet old remembered. Old people always remembered a hotter one from some ancient time like 1950, but we rarely listened to them except politely at Sunday dinner and even then only as long as the dessert and Mom's vigilance lasted. Hot summers were good for corn, but for people the heat and the awful Ohio humidity ate away at you, especially before air conditioning when you had to live in the weather. It was a big, damp towel over everything. The waves of heat and humidity would break with violent thunderstorms, also good for the corn.

I do a lot of remembering on this bus. I was just remembering our old house here in Reeve, Ohio used to have a porch, where Dad and Mom would sit out and drink lukewarm beer. Over the years, the story changed to iced tea or lemonade, but I clearly remember him saying beer often enough and, when I got older, mentioning nips of whiskey from a bottle he kept outside under some cushions for when Mom stepped off the porch to visit with someone. After everybody got their air conditioners, the porch filled with bikes and lawn equipment. Then Mom and Dad, they moved 'cause Dad lost his job, town factory closed down. That was a real sack of it.

"You remember that last summer, the one between junior and senior year?" Muley asked me on the bus. I hadn't talked to him in years, but I quickly was adjusting to talking to long-missing people who happened to be riding my bus. That summer was a while ago, the year the first Star Wars came out and everyone was saying "May the Force be with you" all the time. "Jeez, people still say it now, lame," said Muley. In 1977, a fat and weepy Elvis was dead and we listened to Kiss and Alice Cooper in a not-then-ironic kind of way. We lived in Reeve, Ohio. Reeve isn't really on the way to anywhere, but is located between Clyde and Gibbsville, places people seem to know better, to give you an idea where it was. Not too far from Columbus, the nearest actual really big city.

Muley had one of those smiles that when he got around to grinning would bring you in. He otherwise maintained a kind of glazed look, like school pictures. Sometimes he missed the point, which was part of what made him funny. I remembered swimming in the river with him, a bunch of us really, a couple of days before high school football practice would start. Six packs of Little Kings, where you lost half the beer to foam just opening them in the heat.

"Wait guys, I'm thinking."

"Ah, c'mon Muley, how long is that gonna take?"

"No, seriously, here's this joke," Muley said. "So this family down in one of the south patches has like nine kids and they won't have another, 'cause they heard that one out of ten kids born in America is Mexican, and the mom and dad don't speak Mexican."

"That ain't no joke. My old man says Mexicans are taking away our jobs." That was Rich, the old new kid.

"There aren't hardly any Mexicans in this town. No work for 'em."

"What about that one junior kid?"

"He's the exchange student from Korea somewhere. They don't talk in Spanish over there."

"Well, it's a good thing then, because we need our jobs, my dad says." Rich's dad always said things Rich then said to us.

"My grandfather gets drunk and still talks about the Irish coming into this part of Ohio and taking jobs." My other friend Tim said that. He'll probably get on this bus too before long.

"Your grandfather is some old crapper."

"Why'd you say that? You Irish?"

"I don't know. I was born in Pennsylvania. Am I?" Muley again.

"There's this joke I heard. 'Part of me says I shouldn't be drinking so much' and the other part says 'Don't listen to that drunk.'"

"I don't get it. Why ain't he drinking anymore?" Like I said, sometimes it's funny when Muley doesn't get stuff.

"When's that cut under your nose gonna heal, Muley?" And when Muley didn't get something, Tim was already there like that.

"What cut?"

"He means your dumb mouth, Muley."

"Is that some kind of joke?"

"No, just one of those things, like how come your dad eats cake with a spoon."

"Football practice and school is starting soon," I said. It was on my mind the whole time. It felt like a Sunday night, not looking forward to Monday.

"Senior year we gotta take physics class." Rich again.

"Is that the one with triangles and math?" Muley of course.

"We got almost another month of summer."

"But August goes by faster than July."

It was sometimes fun on the bus to remember those kinds of afternoons. Like all kids, I had no idea if I was livin' in the best of times or the worst, I just lived in the only time there was. We could go on and on like that, talking without saying much, enjoying being young and stupid and irresponsible, warm and happy in the warm brown river water. We were boys.

We didn't yet know about the broken places in life, the dark threads.

I SAY LET the young men in other small Ohio towns dream of bright lights. We didn't need a fortune teller. We knew growing up we were going to work in that factory. We said, "Graduate today, factory tomorrow." Life was rich, fat, happy enough. Hard at the beginning when rough guys looked at you like a puppy who couldn't stay off the couch, hot and full of swear words in between and at the other end you had a pension and on Thursdays free bus rides to the new Atlantic City casinos, box lunch provided. I thought that factory in Reeve where everyone's dad, and grandpa, uncle, brother and cousin worked was drawn in ink but it turned out to be watercolor. When the factory died, I was a Telemarketer. Tire salesman, one McJob after another. Christmas help at the Higbee's, Hill's, Halle's, Uncle Bill's, Giant Tiger, Gold Circle, Lazarus, Clark's department stores that have all since gone belly-up. The development that had been planned for Reeve, the one that was gonna bring in big retail stores and jobs for everyone, fizzled on some complicated six-way derivative financing deal, whatever the hell that even is, and so, long after they tore down the factory, the land stayed vacant.

There were pieces of machinery from the factory left on the ground, too unimportant to sell off, too heavy to move, too bulky to bury, left scattered like clues from a lost civilization, droppings of our failure. Might as well been the bones of the men who worked there. Better than what happened at Youngstown Sheet and Tube, which famously made cannon balls for the North including Ohio during the Civil War, where they left the pig iron making furnace up like a tombstone. At least when a person died they'd close his eyes and throw a blanket over him. Here they just left everything. The last men to work in that plant were the ones who tore out its guts and disassembled the machines. Same as in Weirton, in West Virginia, where my cousin was from. The whole town was built around a single steel mill and when it closed, a good Midwest town died of old age. A local newspaper ran a feature story about one worker, Jack Brown, who made $24.65 an hour in 1982 at the mill and now was unsure if he'd ever find work again. We were once the American Dream, and now we're just what happened to it. I think God owes us an apology.

People said we'd seen this kind of change before. At the time of the American Revolution, we learned in school ninety-five percent of the U.S. population lived on farms. Now it was only two percent. Thing is that those farming jobs were replaced with industrialized jobs, at a ratio of better than one-to-one. Now, with the factory jobs gone and not coming back, rock bottom isn't a destination but an expectation for us. This town used to employ thousands of people, families really, and when the manufacturing jobs went away and weren't replaced they also took with them a way of life. A regime change. What is the purpose of towns that used to have a reason for being and now don't anymore?

A couple of years later things got started again in Reeve during what was then the latest recovery and turnaround and corner turned, and another group of investors moved off the scrap metal and paved the factory site, like a mercy killin'. They then ran out of money and pretty soon the place was home to only itinerant peddlers with velvet paintings and stolen car stereos selling out of the back of vans. A big sigh of relief when they broke ground later for something, what turned out to be only a shitty strip mall. Since nobody in Reeve had much money, the dreams of high-end stores that would take that money ended up being satisfied by some fast-food places, plus a couple of dollar stores run by Koreans who found their way to Reeve God knows how. When I was a kid grandma used to say "Satan can't be everywhere, so he created liquor stores." Amen to that, 'cause there was also a new state store selling LOTTERY LIQUOR CIGS, the three main food groups for us working poor, all the sadness of the town there in those three words (the Ohio state government kept a monopoly on hard liquor sales, they knew their people).

There was also a club with blacked-out windows I'll let on more about later. Plus we had a coffee shop, a little joke from someone who knew unemployed people needed a place to hang out during the day, especially after revenue cuts closed the Carnegie public library with its ivy beard I always liked. Smaller businesses happy to extract smaller amounts of money was our economic rebirth here in Reeve. The town still had its looks, to a point. Old habits die hard. When middle class folks fall out of the middle class, they still tend to keep things neat and see that the grass gets cut. But what was once maybe quaint was now just old.

Riding the bus, I remembered that waiting—time—is the real currency of this new economy. The more money you got, the less you gotta wait. Priority lines, expedient fees, private jets for some, for me, waiting twenty minutes or forty minutes, you never know so better leave early, for a city bus to take you sometime somewhere. Pretty soon you're out here in a parking lot waiting for work from someone with more money but less time than you.

IT HAD RAINED again overnight, puddles rainbowed with oil. March now, which should have been an improvement over February, but in Ohio this year it wasn't, the wet snow and cold rain leaving you thinking Bambi had killed spring or something. Some familiar faces in the parking lot, guys I sorta recognized from way back when I was in high school, maybe the football team, I can't really say—picking out their faces was like tryin' to spot tears in the rain now as an adult. Here they weren't that way no more, a long way from tan and tight-muscled, instead slurry-eyed and tired, sort of hunched over against the cold day, the wind leaning on them. While we sometimes talked, it was about nothing much, safer that way, as you never knew what a guy was carrying around with him that you'd stir up. Some of the guys had already had a few drinks no matter how early it was, some had given up drinking and seemed worse for not having it, some had just plain given up, emptied bottles.

"I need tres hombres, arriba," said the man in the pickup.

"We speak English brother. We're Americans, too."

"Well, yens' are dirty like Mexicans. Anyway, I'm looking for three today."

"What'cha got? Construction? Painting?"

"Three of you wanna work, get in the back of the truck."

"What're you payin'?"

"I'm at $2.50 an hour."

"That ain't minimum wage."

"Did I say $2.50? I meant two bucks an hour. Now, another of you smartasses got a problem, or you like being poor and standing in a parking lot?"

I had had enough.

"If none of us take his shitty $2.50, he'll have to pay us better."

"Shut up, Earl. I'll take your shittin' $2.50 mister."

"Get in the truck, and watch your mouth if you want a job today. And I still am thinking about the $2.50. We'll see how it works out, if you're lazy or not."

13

"Get out of his truck. C'mon, man."

"You go to hell, Earl. I need this."

Two more looked at their feet a bit too long, and I knew we'd been broken. They climbed, silently, into the back of the pickup. The guy driving flipped me off and hit the gas, splashing puddle scum at me, now with another eight hours 'til dark.

The next day we were all back in the lot. Hungry and angry walk pretty close to each other. Puts the bullies up front 'cause regular people stop caring.

"To Hell with you, Earl, man, just to Hell with you. I should've pushed them assholes out and gotten in the truck myself yesterday."

"How much that guy end up paying you all yesterday?"

"We only got the two bucks an hour thanks to your smartass mouth, Earl, but he kept us on for nine hours so we did okay. Bastard had us tearing out insulation, worked every last dollar outta us. We asked for a break and the jerkoff laughed at us, saying, 'What, you in a union?'"

"It sucked but, yeah Earl, you keep your mouth shut next time and we'll at least get some work."

"Don't tell me to shut up, you asshole. You was being used and you're too dumb to even see it."

"Fuck you, Earl. Go find a job with the Koreans movin' into town. Maybe they'll let you clean up their crap for them."

I hadn't hit anyone since junior year of high school, and that was just Muley one time when we got into a fight over some stupid football game neither of us remembered right. There was a lot of trash talk and some pushing and shoving in between long lulled pauses like we saw in movies. I swung at him and

Muley poked me once alongside of my nose and we wrestled a bit. It didn't hurt much more than when you eat ice cream too fast.

This time it was sudden and rough. We were older, hungrier and colder, and there was a lot more on the table than us just calling each other names in the parking lot. The first guy swung sloppily, but caught the side of my head with the punch, and his class ring tore off a part of my scalp. I reached up to touch at the blood and he hit me solid in the nose, starting a finger-width flow of blood down my face. His friend slid in and connected twice on my gut, making me bend over with sour vomit in my mouth. I stood up, dizzy, and tried to put my hands in front of my face, but they all took a couple more shots until I tasted blood over the vomit, and one tooth felt too sharp against my tongue, like it was chipped. I spit up some onto the pavement and that seemed to satisfy them somehow 'cause they stopped hitting me. Only 'cause of the bleeding did I know I was still alive.

"Come here again messing with our work my friend, and you're a dead man. We will freaking wreck your shit, Earl."

They might have been done with me, but they weren't done.

A random passerby.

"Hey, you, you Korean bastard, c'mon over here."

"Yeah, you son-of-a-bitch, come here."

"Bastard is probably on his way to some job he took from one of us."

He came over, saying something in Korean. He didn't seem to understand what was going on.

"Hey slant, you take my job?"

"Why are you even here, you fuck? Go home to Korea."

Language barrier or no language barrier, he figured what he had walked into. He said something else none of us could understand, and turned to leave.

"Hey, you trying to run away? You don't like us? Why don't you like us, you foreign piece of shit?"

"Look, he keeps trying to say something. Speak American you little fuck."

He was scared now. He kept jerking his head at me, I guess 'cause I was the one off to the side and not up in his face, but Christ, look at me. A weak "Leave him alone" was about all I was good for.

"So he's your pal now Earl? You two buddies? You two boyfriends, Earl, that why you're on his side?"

"You little gook shit. We should fuck you up."

He went down pretty hard under the first blows. I couldn't tell if he was hit, or he just crumpled up figuring that was best. Then I saw he had some blood on his mouth, but what really hurt him were those two or three kicks while he was on the ground. One of the guys ripped off his coat by the sleeves and threw it aside. His backpack got tore open and we saw his school books splay out onto the pavement.

"Shit, he's just some school kid. He's probably only in junior high or something."

"You asshole, we just beat the shit outta a little kid. Let's get the fuck outta here before someone calls the fucking cops."

It wasn't the kind of place where anybody would call the cops. Some of the Mexicans lined up also looking for work came over and helped the kid to his feet, and kind of shooed me away.

Them Mexicans had been at the game longer and knew when to keep their distance. I just went back to where I was staying, which wasn't far enough.

MOST THINGS ON the bus were nicer, at least at first. I remembered what my dad would always say to his friend Stan when I was a kid:

"So Stan, how come we never ran into each other when we was serving in Korea?"

"I don't know, maybe because I was in the Air Force and you was in the Army? I flew over the mud and you wallowed in it."

"You weren't in the real Air Force, you were a navigator."

Stan and my dad had done this routine for years, with the ease and confidence of well-practiced behavior. Bob and Ray, Ralph and Alice, Cheech and Chong, Homer and Marge, whoever had been on TV since before I started being more entertained by the ghosts on this bus than the stuff on the screen. It always ended with Stan taking a fake jab at my dad. I guess when they were younger it was like a movie punch, but over the years it had faded into a gesture, more like a half-wave than even an act of pretend violence.

When my dad would entertain us with stories from Korea, usually after a few of, but not all of, what he was drinking that evening, he could be a pretty funny guy. Always sat at the table in his t-shirt, a towel around his neck like he was thinking of sweating hard even at home. The Korean War was his big life experience, his only time outside the U.S. and up until that point pretty much the only non-wedding or funeral trip he'd ever made outside of Reeve. Join the service, he'd tell me, make a man of you, have some fun seeing the world. Best years of his life in Korea. Got blind drunk in Itaewon on black market booze. Ran into some hookers (he said when Mom went inside for another jar of lemonade) and had more fun than $20 should be allowed to buy. Won money in poker Tuesday, lost it all back on Thursday. R&R in Yokohama, too much to talk about with such a sensitive boy's ears around. Didn't fight hardly none at all, sat guard duty on some stupid hill for the whole war, never saw a North Korean, never saw many Koreans out there on that hill at all except some damn beggar kids and their wrinkled up old mamas. "Wouldn't want to touch them women, even for free," he'd say, pausing, then, always to laughs, "or even if they'd a paid me."

He owned one suit, one pair of dress shoes and two watches, always wore the cheap stainless one, never took the gold one from his father out of the drawer except for those weddings and funerals. Said he was saving it, but he died, and I just pawned it. He was the boss at home. "This house is a democracy," he'd say, "but I got 99 of the votes and your mother has the other one. You, son, got none, get used to that." He'd talk about that factory where he worked like some people would talk about God because—along with football—they were all the same in Reeve and you'd no sooner curse one than be damned by them all. The factory took the tip of his left hand index finger by accident, and it was crooked and a mean red when he pointed. Mom always said he was a man of two faces. He had one for daytime, especially with a drink, and another one at night, more purple, especially with another drink. Sometimes his meanness was

18

almost casual, and sometimes it was like a tough ass dog let off the leash.

Me and Dad had not done a lot of talking, and as he got older the reasons for us not to talk fell away, though the habit of not talking stayed. I'd call home from wherever I was looking for work, and his way of answering the phone was to say, "Here's your mom."

I remember one Saturday in a December when I was maybe ten or so. It snowed overnight, a Midwest blast of twelve or fourteen inches all within a couple of hours, shutting down the Twentieth Century in Reeve. Every kid poured outside that morning and we built huge snow forts, great walls to rival that one in China, and a street-wide snowball war erupted. With nothing on TV because we had no electricity, the dads came out to see what was going on, and before we knew it, had joined into the snowball throwing. There must have been twenty men and their sons out there hurling wet snow, except one. I remember running into the house, the snow melting off me while my mom yelled about the mess, me crying, begging my old man to come out. He just said, "No snowballs for me, seen enough snow in Korea to last forever," and laid down on the couch. My mom shooed me back outside, looking over at Dad, saying he needed to rest more, even though he'd just got up. My tears came down either side of my nose and outside froze in place and I can almost still feel them pinching. Even after I caught one snowball right in the nose and started to bleed, I wouldn't go home that day.

He'd whoop me when I was little, usually 'cause of what he called my "goddamn disrespectful mouth," them three words said as one slur. He hit me like he'd never stop, then one day when I was about eight or nine he just stopped, like something grabbed his hand, held his fist and he never hit me again after that, not once, I never knew why. You remember the things from childhood that scare you and I'll never forget that.

I never knew him to pick me up when I was a kid, "Not his way, but he loves you all the same," Mom would say, but as he aged I grew bitter at the loss of something never there, and when he did try and hug me like he saw the other old people around him do when I visited as an adult, I pulled back. We tried unsuccessfully a few times to patch things, but re-sew it over and over, you always can see the tear. Dad was never one of those dads that supposedly went out for a pack of smokes and never came home. No, he didn't abandon his family when things got messed up, but he'd sure as hell expect that we'd adjust to him. "I got to go to work, you know, so be quiet and don't get upset when I miss your game or raise a hand at your mother," he'd say. Mom one time created this big deal where as a kid I was supposed to watch him shave, some father-son thing, but as soon as she left the bathroom he just said, "I shave every morning, don't see what the big goddamn deal is," so I just went back to Mom in the kitchen. He left his mark on me like a thumbprint pressed into wet plaster, but I never knew how when we never even talked.

My mom was named something else, but everyone called her Sissy, after her being the only sister in a big family of brothers. That summer between junior and senior year I remember a lot, but it was only after my mom started getting on the bus with me that it started to make sense to me as an adult. It seemed there was always more between her and Dad than I could see, like they played parts called "Mom" and "Dad" in front of me, but were different people with each other. Mom said Dad loved her and that was important for me to know, but that it was a Midwest kind of thing where he loved her almost enough to tell her.

It occurred to me that maybe Mom had it right, or at least saw it all coming sort of unconsciously. She waitressed at the Lenny's, now part of a big nationwide chain of diners, but the place used to be Anthony's Café, where food came in "baskets" or as "platters," and old guys sat at the counter bent over coffee like bowed tree limbs. It was owned by Big Tony, then his son Little Tony, who died, and his own son who wasn't named Tony sold it to the Lenny's company, which is now owned by Dubai investors who can't find Ohio on a map. A thing owning a thing. Before it was sold, the Tony's used to put up hand-written signs all over the place, saying things like NO CHECKS with the NO in red and underlined twice or WE DON'T LOOK IN YOUR MOUTH, SO YOU DON'T LOOK IN OUR KITCHEN. Waitresses said "Here you go," dropping off food, and asked, "Still working on it?" midway, and "Any room for dessert?" at the end, which was what good service was in a place like that. Didn't call people "Honey," that was just at the Waffle Houses further south. Mom waitressed, mostly for tips, serving meals to people who paid using dollars they earned selling shoes made in Sri Lanka to people who made a living being personal trainers to other people who earned their living buying and selling bonds and stocks. Nobody made nothing, except maybe the cooks who broke eggs for omelets. Poultry was always big in this part of Ohio.

❧   ❧   ❧

MOM REMEMBERED SOME things to me on the bus:

"I invited Lori and Stan over next weekend, Ray. I figured we could play cards or something."

"That'd be fine," said Ray.

Ray was my dad—Mom called him Ray when they talked and I wasn't around.

"By the way, Sissy, what the hell happened to the grass out front? It's all torn up."

"I think Earl and his friends were tossing around the football, might have got a little rough I guess."

"I spend too much time on that lawn for him to just rip it up like that."

"Well, we're raising a boy, not grass."

"Got bad news at the factory today."

That's when I walked through. Dad shot me a look, like I shouldn't have come in right then.

"How's that, Ray?"

"Seems that foreman job they was talking about, they're gonna give it to some guy they're gonna bring in from Columbus."

"Well, maybe next round, Ray. You know, as long as Earl's here now, I know he had something he wanted to talk to us—"

"Mom—"

"He wants to talk more about that football scholarship. Maybe go to college. He talked to me about it a lot last night, Ray."

"Football's one thing but school's another, huh Earl?" said Dad, his mouth now full of food mixed with beer from the bottle that I swear was sewn onto his hand at meals. It was then that I stomped out, making each wooden step on the staircase moan as I hit them hard, all the way up. There were days that Mom and Dad must have thought stomping on the floor was the only way we had left to communicate, like cave men or something. That house did have solid floors, though.

Just Mom and Dad down there now.

"You thought about what we were talking about last night?" asked Dad.

"You mean me quittin' my job?"

"Uh-huh. I figured you'd, um, you know, want more time to yourself," Dad said, "that's all. I talked to Stan yesterday afternoon while you were out. His wife just quit her job."

"And that's what you'd want me to do, just so you'd feel better? Ray, I told you when I took that job it was because I had to. People keep worrying about the factory, and you heard the house on the end just went to the bank. Them people been living there for fifteen years and now it's like one of those old sad movies around here. I keep seein' men with suits knock on a door, and then nothing good happens to a family."

"Well, we could have another yard sale, sell off some of this junk you bought," said Dad.

"Ray, nobody wanted the broken stereo or the crock pot or the things from the garage that went with the old car. We sold some of Earl's baby stuff to those out-of-towners only because they thought they was funny old things. For that $15 I lost the Golden Books I read to him over and over them nights you worked double shifts while the factory still had overtime for you. Was that worth that $15? 'Cause everythin' else that was sold was just neighbors being polite, pawing through what we had and touching everything and then buying a Tupperware for ten cents 'cause it was cheaper than saying no. I ended up buyin' stuff from them two weeks later just keepin' relations. Some people even stole stuff when I went inside. That how you wanna live now?"

"Dammit Sissy, stop nagging me—"

"Ray, it's changing."

"Sissy—"

"You know the refrigerator is making a wheezing sound and even on sale at Sears they're expensive. Wages at the factory keep going down for ya'll, them saying we have to share the sacrifice to keep the company afloat. I even heard of a family sleeping nights in their car now over in Gibbsville, kids in the back seat while the old man tries to get some sleep for work the next day. That for us, Ray?"

"I think we're a ways from being like Gibbsville and all that Sissy. Factory been here in Reeve a long time, and I'm one of the senior men on shift. Settle yourself down and stop worrying. Makes you get wrinkles. Hell, my father raised a family outta that factory. We make glass at that factory Sissy, we aren't made of it you know. I'll always have something."

For a long time I never understood economics, just lopping it in with the math I hated in high school. When was we ever going to use this stuff, we'd say, plodding through the equations. I remember those words and I remember the hours in the classrooms and how hot it always seemed, but I could not figure out how long one side of a triangle is knowing the other dimensions and other than Muley asking me how high a flag was once when we took a field trip to Greenfield Village in

Dearborn, Michigan, and me knowing the answer had something to do with measuring the shadow. I told Muley I didn't know and who cared anyway how tall the flag pole was, stupid question.

The joke's on you, Mr. Donovan, we really never did need to use that math stuff. How many hours me and Muley sat in there, staring out the window at spring passing us by, waiting for them classes to end. School didn't mean much to us 'cause we all knew the future. We'd work in the factory here in Reeve like our daddy done because that was the way of it. Nobody's dad made that much more or less than everyone else's dad. There was no 99 percent in Reeve then, as we was all one hundred percent 99 percent. But it worked. Muley had an above ground pool and the summer before my old man bought a new Buick LeSabre. Things were right the way they were between the factory and the men. They needed each other. It was a kind of team.

As I got older and more unemployed though, I came to understand that economics was less about math and more about people, and how we lived. The economic word "flexibility" came in my lifetime to be a stand-in for lower pay and fewer benefits. The system had been in place for my grandpa and my dad: Put something into the factory and get something back from the factory. Giving and getting were intimately related. There are rich men and working men, and rich men always have more but working men have enough. It was like a contract, and we saw it every day in Reeve. Like a marriage, it wasn't always good and I ain't romanticizing it. Some men left hands and fingers in those machines like my dad did, and both sides might cheat a bit on the other. But it worked well enough, and well enough was about what most of us wanted.

This used to be a country that talked about dreams with a straight face. Now we keep the old myth alive that America is some special good place, but in fact we're just like some mean old man, reduced to feeling good about himself by yelling at the kids. In Reeve, that was Mr. Voriski. He'd always be upset about anyone stepping on his grass, or a ball bouncing into his yard. Sometimes he'd come out shouting with a baseball bat, or, in some versions, a shotgun (though repeated by generations of high school kids, no one ever actually saw a gun, but many older brothers' friends did). Nobody respected old man Voriski, even after we found out he was a war refugee or was some survivor of something or another. We stayed off his lawn because he had that baseball bat, nothing more. What's so surprising is how quickly it all changed. America went from big empty space to king of the world in a handful of generations. The generations that lived this dream we keep hearing about could fit at a weekend family reunion, but we keep talking about them like they lasted longer than the dinosaurs.

MOM ON THE bus with me:

Your dad always said he loved you, but that he left the parenting work to me. He'd bring home the money we needed, do some chores on Saturday and fall asleep on the couch every Sunday afternoon, and consider that his obligations were fulfilled. He never once took you to the dentist, went to a parent-teacher conference or watched you try on new school clothes. It had worked for us for a long time, that system, and me having to go to work was not an easy thing, especially me working as a waitress where the neighbors could see. Even though I hadn't been at it long, some days it felt like I was doing it since coffee was a dime. "You done Sissy? Goin' home?" people would say to me and I'd answer "Yep, gotta get supper on the table." I carried a lot of food around those days.

We'd been married long enough that a whole world could pass between us in a look. You were upstairs in your room with the door slammed shut forever. I knew we would not see you again until you got hungry, so I stopped talking and started to give him that kinda smile. You're old enough to know these things now, Earl honey. At first he gave me back that look that reminded me of when I married him. So I hopped into your dad's lap, and he faked being surprised by my weight on him. I kissed him on the lips.

"Remember," I said to him, "that summer after we just got married, before Earl was born, we'd spend all day Sundays in bed? We'd just be there, taking time to read the funny papers in between, the rest of the newspaper spread over the bed like a blanket. Next thing we'd know it'd be dark and dinner time? One Sunday all we ate the whole day was Pop Tarts and pretzels, kissin' the crumbs off each other."

Your dad wasn't smiling no more. His gaze was somewhere across the room.

"C'mon," I said, gesturing upstairs. Earl won't notice."

Your dad did not say anything, just looked away, then back at me. I ignored him, then stood up as I began to understand. "Don't it change?" I said. Then there was a long pause as I looked harder at him. He snapped his glance back towards me, but I turned away and got up to rattle the coffee pot around. I went and just set a bowl and spoon in front of him and turned back to the stove. Times like that I looked at your father like the mom with the town's slow kid watching the other boys and girls run and play around the pool. Wasn't nice. Wasn't womanly. Wasn't manly.

After that, I went on to see Lori, your dad's friend Stan's wife that afternoon, wanting out of that house.

"Stan says you're gonna quit your job," Lori said. "He heard Ray is gonna ask you to quit. I tell you, me and Stan have gotten along much better since I left work. At first we figured the extra money would be nice, but then Stan and I started fighting all the time and it wasn't worth it to me. He kept telling me all this crap about how his mother never had to work. Well, I told him his father worked for the old R.H. Reeve Company factory, but that didn't faze him one bit. So I quit. It's better now, better I guess. Anyways, how's Earl? I saw him the other day. He came by looking for Rob."

"He did?"

"Yeah, 'cept Rob was still working. He's still getting over losing that scholarship chance to play at Ohio State. Making decent starting money at the factory though, so it ain't all bad."

We was taking a walk, and Lori caught the toe of her shoe on an uneven section of the sidewalk.

"Sissy, you keep a secret?"

"Sure, a' course Lori."

"Um, you and Ray thinkin' of another kid?"

"No. I mean, no, not just right now. Ray, see, well, it's not easy to say, but. . ."

"Sissy, I'm late."

"Really? You and Stan happy about that?"

"I'm thinking we are. I mean, sure, we are."

"You alright Lori?"

"I'm okay."

"Lori, does Stan yell at you?"

"Like when he's mad about dinner?"

"No, no, like just because he's mad about something but you can't figure what it is."

"Sometimes. Sometimes he's just angry. Something gets angry inside of him. Like bad food or something grumbling in there. Just angry. Ya know Sissy?"

"I do. I do know."

YOUR DAD AND I went to where I worked, for dinner, 'cause I got an employee discount. He was trying to make nice with me that night and knew going out to eat would help. We started well enough being just polite but finished the meal in silence. Sometimes after you been married a while you just run out of things to say, need to rest up. That's okay. The waitress brought over the check. Your Dad inspected it, then put it back down on the table. I picked up the check and re-added it out of waitressin' habit, my lips moving slowly as I concentrated. I reached into my purse for the money and handed it to your dad like he liked me to do. I was trying too to make nice.

"Well, thanks for a fine meal," he said, winking at the waitress behind the register. "Just like home." She smiled and counted out change. Your dad pocketed it, walked out, and we had to argue again.

"But you work there."

"Ray, please."

Your dad handed me the change. I walked in and put a tip on the table, avoiding the other waitresses as I passed through the room, wishing I was a ghost. I was hoping they thought he'd just forgot it but they probably just remembered the last time when he must've forgot too. But I stayed quiet about it, like I thought a real ghost might.

I REMEMBERED, SITTING there on the bus, that my dad came up to my room that night, after they'd come home.

"Your mother says we should have a talk about this football scholarship business. I don't know really what to say. Chances of you getting it coming out of Reeve are pretty slim, so don't get your hopes up. Look what happened to Rob, ending up at the factory and all after failing tryouts at Ohio State. You should get something to fall back on. Your mother's gonna quit her job soon and it wouldn't hurt you to start contributing to this house."

"Yeah, I know."

"Yeah, I know you know. You heard all this a thousand times from me."

That all counted as a typical kind of conversation, and his last words as almost an apology, for, I don't know, him being him.

He was always short with me, a lot of times cutting off just about anything, saying, "Well, I'm tired, just got back from work" or "Got to go to work now." I don't know he'd have had anything to say at all without that job.

THE FACTORY WAS a hard breathing place. It was where almost every man worked, it was Reeve's biography and we all knew it, even the men who could not talk about much of what they thought. Sometimes people forget that even though you speak with an accent you don't think with one, and most of Reeve's men did their share of thinking about that factory. It was that factory that made Reeve until the late 20th century, and then unmade it throughout the rest. It sat near the river, but the two no longer mattered to one another, grown apart people said like in a divorce. Reeve in fact was built near—because of—a river, like Detroit, like Pittsburgh, like Louisville, even Chicago, which was in the right place but needed a different river so they just dug one. Things were different in those days, people more willing to do things like make the Chicago River flow the other way because they needed that. The rivers then were needed for transportation of raw materials like iron from the Northeast and for shipping finished goods down the Mississippi. The rivers provided power, and water to cool the factory machines. Now, a town existing because of a river seemed as out of place as a typewriter, a phone with a cord, a two-parent family.

Today's Reeve came about because of the factory like I said, originally the R.H. Reeve Company, owned and begun by the Reeve family to make glass insulators for the power lines that were poking fingers west behind the railroads. Early on there was also some coal, long since mined out. A few of the hills in town actually started life as slag heaps, slate pulled away from the coal and discarded before anyone knew about fracking. Anyway, things soon turned discarded for the factory, too. The world stopped needing glass insulators as Bakelite and then plastic became available, and the factory changed to making glass things in molds, all kinds of things people needed like drinking glasses and cooking stuff. Those were good times for Reeve, really starting to accelerate after World War II was won and Grandpa came home to a factory job, and then as my father was working at the factory from as soon as he returned from the Korean War right up until the factory first went out of business in the late 1970s. Luckily, some Japanese investors bought it and converted half the men to unemployed and the other half to making new glass things people needed more than cookware, television picture tubes, though at lower wages than before to "save jobs."

This seemed at first to be Reeve's lucky break, TV picture tubes. Most of the manufacturing process was automated, technology over craft in a vital signal we all missed. A decent number of jobs to work the furnaces and handle the raw materials. Glass was good for this kind of item, and we all looked around and knew that people would always want TVs and so they'd need what we were making. The factory sold to American television makers, stable companies like RCA, Motorola and Magnavox. We did not adjust well to the rise of flat-screen LED TVs without the old vacuum picture tubes, never even saw it coming. Wages fell, and then the jobs went away altogether as we became part of the Rust Belt. That name even became a short-hand way to sum up the loss of an entire way of life—oh, he got caught up in the Rust Belt.

The factory was then bought by some hedge fund owned by someone, who used the factory's physical assets to issue junk bonds defaulted on as the hedge fund moved its reserves offshore to wherever the hell the Cayman Islands are to take advantage of tax breaks created by a president most people in Reeve never voted for. In return, that president never asked us what that tax law decision might do to Reeve. Last I heard, the old factory area was owned by a European consortium more interested in the land for retail development. Ain't nothing made in factories no more, least not in Ohio. There ain't no jobs for anyone coming home either, though we have had several new wars during all these times for men to come home from. A thousand people a day used to walk into that factory to make a living. Now those streets could just be stage sets for some end-of-the-world germ virus movie. Hard to build a town, a life, when the best business is done at the Bowl America, $2.25 a bottle for Lite beer. Rock bottom ain't a foundation.

Reeve then worked according to certain principles. And this ain't nostalgia, it's history. A steak should be one inch thick or more. You figure out how to mind your own business and help your neighbor at the same time. A good potluck can solve most problems. Vegetables were boiled. Faith was rewarded. Things'll look better in the morning. Three channels of broadcast TV defined the cultural high water mark. It was a big deal the first Fourth of July when your dad let you set off fireworks on your own. You were allowed to let a younger brother burn his fingers once by encouraging him to hold a burning sparkler too long, like had been done to you. We still had parades, every Memorial Day and every July Fourth, but Labor Day was just for barbecues because school began the next day and Dad had to get up for work. "I've got to get up for work" was the way most social events broke up, as committal a goodbye as pulling the plug on the music and putting the rugs back down on the floor. On holidays, time was measured more by "just had lunch" or "getting toward supper." We were neither a small town nor a suburb, we were what was a common thing in this part of Ohio. We had a Dairy Queen, a Catholic school and four Protestant churches. Bowl America was the body heat of Reeve, where the men all got together to drink after telling their wives they were going bowling. The older guys didn't even bother to leave the house with a ball, it was such a pattern of their lives. Once upon a time in this town you could ask someone the time, and they'd say "Why?" Work was controlled by the factory whistle and the sun, and both were controlled by God and equally vital. You did work from one to the other.

Reeve could be reduced down to this: I was a boiler operator. So was my dad. Went to work every day but Thanksgiving, Christmas, New Years, and two weeks of summer. Bought a car. Bought a house. Sent one son to college, gave one to the Marine Corps. Have a decent pension. Living quietly now in that same house. Own it.

That is how it was in 1977. Now, grassroots is Astroturf and I'm unemployed and unskilled and riding a bus all day. I am part of the one third of all working Americans who are "contingent." We are part-timers or day laborers or freelancers or franchisees or temps or independent contractors or on call. I clean floors and stock warehouse shelves and deliver things you buy on-line and serve you food. I don't have health insurance. I get sick, I don't work, a bull whose balls have given out. I don't get paid extra for working overtime or holidays because an hour is an hour no matter when I work it and I am not eligible for unemployment because I technically never had a real job in the first place to be unemployed from.

A lot of days I didn't work at all. The tough one was always Sunday with nothing but an unemployed Monday ahead. That's the one that made you think, the one that hurt. If you could get past Monday morning, the rest of the unemployed week fell into place. When I get too old to be unemployed I'll become retired and unemployed. I got a lot of free time, but no real weekends or time off to enjoy, 'cause it ain't dessert without the supper first. I make too much for food benefits, but I fucking hate canned tuna and cereal for dinner. I allow companies to be flexible and nimble over my dead body.

Sorry, sometimes on this bus, thinking this over, I get a little stirred up. Good news that Muley was back on the bus. I liked it best with him riding along.

MULEY SAID TO me:

Earl, you remember that one field trip we took to that "living history" Greenfield Village museum place near Detroit? Man, that was great. That bus ride was like a thousand hours, and we was sipping whiskey out of a Coke can the whole time and Mr. DeSalvo never had a clue we was so juiced up. Maybe he wondered when we kept asking when the next pee stop was, but he never let on. And we dared Donny to try and spit out the window and Jeanne told on us before he could? That Greenfield Village place was stupid though. I never seen so much old stuff before, piled-up factory equipment and old trains an' shit like all that was important. You remember the old guy that guided us around? He was so serious about all that "Here's where America's industrial might was born" and "Gaze at these examples of how the American worker won the war for the United States" and "Here's the Model T, the car that changed America," like we cared that Henry Ford raised his workers' pay so they could buy the stupid old cars they built. About the only good thing was we got to stay in a hotel, and we saw Tina Barker in only her bra through the window when we snuck out after curfew. The worst part was in that second museum. "Here's a Gothic Steam Engine. This 30-foot-tall engine drove machinery used to make lead sheet flashing," whatever the hell that was. Man, that was like when we used to have to go to the library to copy stuff out of encyclopedias for our school reports instead of copying it off the Internet like kids do now. Dead stuff from dead men. Who cares, right?

That's what Muley said. For me, I believed then what my dad told me. My dad believed what they told him, but it wasn't true even long enough for his lifetime to last. Day's work for a day's pay, all that country and western calloused hands stuff. Maybe it started out that way for Grandpa, maybe for Dad for a while, but if it was ever true, it ain't no more. I think the bastards made it all up. Instead now, we're back to being sharecroppers. And I ride this bus listening to Rage Against the Machine and trying to remember why I'm so angry all the time. I know I got this ball of anger inside me, growing like a baby, maybe a tumor, a big angry zit of meanness. I can't remember too many things anymore. I can't remember who the hell the Tom Joad guy is that Rage sings about, though the name sticks in my head, maybe somebody I knew from high school.

MY OLD MAN'S best friend was Stan. He was always nice enough to me, so it wasn't surprising to see him on the bus, too. Why not, right?

Stan said to me:

Me and your dad would almost always have a beer or three after work. It was a part of the day really. Go to work, finish work, stop at Bowl America, go on home. They could have put another time clock inside there and we'd not have thought twice about it.

"You comin' in with us?"

"Nah, the little woman's expecting me home."

"Ah, married life."

"Yeah, married life."

We all laughed. It didn't matter that it wasn't so funny, or that we tended to repeat the same lines and retell the same jokes. We laughed because we were supposed to laugh. It was our way of getting along. Inside the bar we drank beer. They had all those bottles of liquor on the shelf behind the bar like they was supposed to have, but I don't recall anyone drinking anything but beer.

"Got the car runnin' yet?"

"Almost. Needs a new clutch plate. Maybe a whole trans. Gonna try to get in it myself to save a few bucks. Borrowed the tools already from Schronbrunner."

"I'll help you. Done it twice, second time it even worked."

"You seen that new girl workin' in the front office?"

"Somethin', huh?"

"Only thing that gets me into work each morning."

"What gets you home?"

"I gotta get going. See you guys."

"Where're you headed, Ray?"

"Home. Where else?"

"Time to get to the old lady."

"In more ways than one, right, Ray?"

"I guess, Charlie. I'll see you Monday."

"Yeah, take care, Ray."

I WALKED OUTSIDE the bar with your dad.

"Well hey there, Ray."

"How you doing, Stan?"

"Days getting shorter, you know Ray? Used to stay light past nine."

"So how's your boy doing, Stan?"

"Rob's pretty happy at the factory after what happened at Ohio State. Would have been a good halfback, maybe make first string after a year if they'd give him a pass on the schoolwork part. But, that's that. Anyway, he's already making $5.60 an hour at the factory. Hey, you know, Rob figures your boy'll be going off somewhere to play ball after his senior year."

"You think Earl's that good, huh?"

"Me and Rob both do."

Your dad and me both looked at our shoes, scraping little patterns in the dirt.

"It was a long day."

"Yeah, I know. You looking forward to tomorrow night?"

"The card party at our house? Damn, Sissy is all fired up about that. I guess we gotta make nice and play along."

"Lori's been bitchin' about never getting out anymore since she quit her job, so yeah, we're gonna be there."

Your old man sometimes picked at the missing tip of his finger. Helped him think. That's when I knew he had something to say I was gonna need to listen to.

"Hey Stan, we had us a pretty good time a couple of weekends ago, driving up to Columbus to see that Triple-A ball team, having a few drinks afterwards, didn't we?"

"Yeah, almost like we was trying to, er, liquidate our assets. I know we got home safe 'cause we're here, but damn if I can remember it all."

"I remember two certain young ladies from the bar."

"That I do recall. Professionals for sure, but damn sweet."

"Fallen women who looked like they needed to be picked up."

"You're a funny guy Stan."

"Ray, the blonde in the sweater vest liked you I think."

"Stan, they all like you as long as you got the do-re-mi in your wallet. But we was good boys, right? Bought 'em a few drinks, sure, but kept our hands to ourselves."

"Yep, that's right Ray. We're married men. I think we both wanted to, but I wouldn't and you couldn't, am I right?"

That was supposed to be funny. But your old man didn't laugh. He stopped drawing things in the dirt and planted both feet.

"Calm down Ray. I was just kiddin'."

"Like hell, you son of a bitch. I told you 'bout me and Sissy's personal problem in confidence, as my friend. Damn you Stan, damn you."

"Give it a break Ray."

"No, you go to Hell Stan."

"If I'm going to Hell, Ray, it'll be you there first waiting for me."

IT WAS EASY for me to remember, riding around on the bus. That was sorta my job nowadays anyway, remembering stuff as people got on and off. But the best thing I can remember was the summer before senior year that I first met Angela, Angel sometimes, usually Angie. Angie insisted for a while that she was named after the Rolling Stones song, which of course meant that she would have had to been renamed in 1973, 'cause she was already thirteen years old when that song came out, but with Angie you accepted these things even if you didn't understand them. Angie was a fibber sometimes but teenage sweet and sincere in her fibs, and had a way that'd let her get past you with anything. She made a big deal outta crossing her sevens, wrote bad poetry and was the first kid in school to try what we thought were drugs (caffeine pills from a rest stop café that just made her stay up all night and pee). She read books, not just for school.

Green eyes as green as the old kind of Christmas tree lights that could start fires. Angie, she could criticize monotony with a clear conscience.

Of course, she was more mature than the rest of us, hell, making fart sounds with our armpits still cracked us up, so it did not take much. Angie was from Cleveland, a big, far away and exotic place to us in Reeve. She read books, not just for school. Her dad had been killed in an accident there, working on the high steel constructing the office buildings that was still being built then, and her mom, originally from Reeve, moved back when she inherited the family home. But when I first met Angie her dad was still alive and she was just visiting her grandparents in Reeve. Me and Muley talked her up one day at the city pool, and when I saw her again the next day I said, "Me and my friend was the guys who talked to you yesterday," and she said, "I don't remember your friend, but you can keep me company." We went on to spend afternoons at the Dairy Queen, and at the end of the summer she asked me something no one ever had before, to write down my mailing address. She said it was a romantic thing to do, to write letters. I had no idea about this and was surprised two weeks later when Mom said I had mail. Angie wrote inside a card, like a birthday card we knew but this one didn't have nothing already printed inside, not store bought words but stuff she thought of. She said the "sun shines for me today" and drew some flowers and signed it Molly "Bloom," I guess because of the flowers.

I dreamed about her, regular dreams and, you know, those kind of dreams. My head was full of her, playing on every station. When dreaming wasn't enough, then I knew I missed her. I carried her card around until it got dirty and sweaty from being pushed and pulled in and out of my pocket. I didn't know what to do. After days of worrying about this, I bought a post card at Schottenstein's Drug Store, which became Discount Drug and Market before it became a CVS and now a DrugCoMart, currently owned by an investor group from Singapore that hires people to find places like Reeve on a map so they can buy more things when old men like Schottenstein die. I worked there for a while, almost a rite of passage during high school, pulling in about four bucks an hour stocking shelves alongside my friends. Our girlfriends ran the registers, our moms and dads shopped in the store and a good story about a date could get you a night off from the sympathetic manager. When someone graduated, the manager would hire one of the workers' friends and the cycle continued.

I asked Angie once, "What do you want to be when you grow up?" and she answered "Do I have to grow up?" She said she didn't want to borrow someone else's dreams, she wanted her own, going everywhere she'd never been until she'd been everywhere. I never knew what to say back, but I liked listening to what she said.

After she moved back to Reeve, we fell in hard with each other, firing up almost without effort together, a camp fire that hadn't been put out and just walked away from. I'm not sure what she saw in me, though it was a good postcard I had selected to send back to her that first summer, one with a picture of a giant rabbit that said BIG THINGS ARE HAPPENING HERE IN REEVE, so that might have helped. It was like texting nowadays but on paper and slower. Must've scratched her right where she itched.

So then I told Angel we were like Romeo and Juliet, which was the most romantic thing me and Muley could come up with from the library. Don't know why the old librarian looked at us so weird when we asked together for the most romantic book. It was a stupid library anyway.

"No, we're not Romeo and Juliet," said Angel. "My dad's dead and my mom just chases around replacing him with a new guy every week. Your mom's a broken robot and your dad's drunk into a coma. None of them give a twist about us."

Which I did not fully understand, but Angel kept on holding my hand, so I guess nodding along was the right move.

I said, "Sometimes I feel awkward when I talk, I don't always know what to say."

"So why talk?" was the way Angie replied.

Then I said to her, "You're beautiful," and she said, "What?" She laughed and told me she heard me clear enough, but just wanted to make me say it again. When I first wanted to kiss her, I was scared, not sure, so I asked if it was okay. She said I shouldn't have asked, I should have just done it. That's how things were with Angie. I mean, we were still kids, and I tasted Dentyne when we kissed. But we told each other we were in love, and I'm pretty sure we were. It was a new thing to me, but you don't always need know a thing, to have seen a thing before, to know it. Some things just are. I understood there was so much I didn't know, but those nights Angie made me believe what I felt. We'd go out under the black umbrella of night and sit as close to the Baltimore and Ohio line as we dared, and when the diesel coalers came past she'd pull me down on her so's I could feel her breasts and she'd scream as loud as she could as the train carried past, saying she could feel my heart even then, pounding, and I'd kiss her like I was trying to pull her heart into me with the generosity of all that moment and I'd hold her like mine were the arms of God themselves. After those nights I'd feel tired way past sleep, but I never wanted to sleep, not 'cause I wasn't exhausted, but because being awake was so good. Lying by the railroad tracks, looking up at the sky, I said, "It all seems so big," and Angie said, "Ain't big enough."

One time she said, "I want to count all your freckles. Can we spend the afternoon doing that?" We did.

I am a little shy to admit I was an educated virgin. There wasn't much to do in Reeve and so we had to make our own fun, and in that respect virginity wasn't innocence as much as simple lack of experience. You had to be flexible in a small town, however, 'cause it was always that you liked the pretty ones and the less pretty ones liked you. My first, second, and several subsequent times were with girls from school, rude jabs in someone's car or after church outside in the woods fooling we were Adam and Eve, but the good part, us all sticky with apple juice, summer's a messy collection of drips, explosions and squirts like I was a hyperactive Irish Setter, my tongue foraging inside some girl's mouth. Most sex then was more of a struggle than a pleasure of its own, as teenage boys and patience do not fit. Looking back, I think the first time I ever had sex inside, not counting cars and vans, I was already twenty-five years old. Our version of an STD was poison ivy. I ended up with a lot of terrible songs burned into the part of my brain that memorized everything around some big event, so the opening chords of "Smoke on the Water" and Debbie Radnick's tube top are forever paired, God bless them both.

One time I forgot to throw out the rubber, the old kind too, the ones that smelled like a new shower curtain, and my dad found it the next day on the car floor like a skin some snake shed. "Don't get no one pregnant or you'll have to get married," he told me, ignoring the obvious thing that I'd used a condom. Me and those girls were certainly never in love, but there was always a little affection as we snorted and rutted, a kinda desperate fun at worst, me laying on 'em like I was protecting them from flying shrapnel, so full of teenage hard up some days I'm embarrassed to say I would've fucked mud, and I kissed a lot of girls.

With Angie it was different. Hell, it was always different. We did a lot of what the health education books in gym class called "heavy petting." This was sincere lust, but it was also a kind of testing. With other girls the testing was more like taking her temperature, seeing if she was willing, trying first base not because it felt like melted chocolate electricity to tongue kiss but mostly to see if you thought she'd let you get under her Peter Frampton t-shirt later. The girls knew it, knew their role in the game, and must've talked among themselves about who to let do what when, 'cause when we boys talked amongst ourselves it all seemed that what we was getting was the same as everyone else. Except James, who was going steady with Evelyn I think since when we still took naps in school. Evelyn unsnapped her bra just to change her mind, and James got her pregnant junior year and his dad had to pay for them to get an apartment and then find him a job at the factory.

But with Angie it was all fun; lust born from love instead of the opposite. She always seemed to indicate she'd go all the way right then and there, but wouldn't it be more fun to look around some. I never felt dirty, never felt that I was taking something or being given something like with them other girls. Even when another girl would signal it was okay, she'd still offer up a hand job so she could appear, you know, reluctant and not seem like some tramp. I never saw the way things could be something other than some kinda job until much later.

So with Angie it felt natural and good and warm when we went to a place in the woods together. I had known the place since I was a kid, a worn spot next to a field, surrounded by blackberry bushes except for one small space you could crawl through like a tunnel. Blackberry bushes have tiny thorns, but lots of them, and pull at clothes and pinch your skin, so you don't want to try and bull through them. When I was littler we caught grasshoppers there in the field, holding them in our cupped hands 'til they spit what we called tobacco juice, all brown and sticky and we had to let them go.

The ground was hard underneath us, Ohio clay baked into rock through a dry June, mingling just a little dust with our sweat into an odor I can summon up on this bus and make myself smile. Heat piled up in that time in Ohio like snow accumulated in December. As kids I played soldiers in there, looked at Tim's dad's Playboys in there and on a lot of nights I took Angie there. I remember every kiss, every time I touched her, the way her hair smelled up close in the sun when I pressed my nose into it, the way her tongue was bright orange from the Cheetos we ate.

Bras in my youth were complex, heavy elastic and nylon evil things with hooks and clasps and wires to struggle against while the girl waited to see if you could, but Angie just that night reached back with one hand and changed all that too in my mind. Looking at the faint red lines left on her, I never got to second base faster or easier, and I never felt stupider again for thinking of it as second base. She had shoulders, soft curves I was pretty sure I never noticed on girls before. Boys is all about parts, boobs and butts and legs and hips like a bucket of fried chicken being divided up, but Angie changed my eyes. She taught me to trace the outline of her with my hands like a whisper, a breeze, one finger, my tongue, always saying slower, softer, let's enjoy the trip. God, I could drink a whole bottle of her.

I thought I knew what to do, indeed had had some significant practice alone (99 percent of people do and the other one percent lie about not doing it) and with girls by that point, but the more I pressed with the urgency of having 99 percent testosterone in my bloodstream the more Angie would move slower, press back softer, remind me we had hours until curfew and that we were sixteen and naked and alone together, slowly and perfectly. Her skin was so warm it scalded me. She held out the rubber in her cupped hands, like we used to do with the grasshoppers. I lost the push-pull and melted into her, and as quickly started to apologize for how I was over and she just smiled and said, "Well, you sweet boy, we'll just have to do it again. It's not fattening." I have no more powerful image not messed up by a photograph available to me after fifty-two years and nor would I want one. I couldn't help thinking this was as close to Heaven as I was ever gonna get, things so warm I hadn't yet dreamed of them.

I wasn't sure what it was that I smelled, but it was familiar growing up around Mom at home, them things in the bathroom waste can, a little sweet and a little coppery, not typical among blackberry bushes but not entirely out of place or something worth slowing down because of. I found her. I heard a song in my head, *So, play on, I'll dance for you.* Angie took my finger in her mouth, I felt her tongue, warm, and she whispered to me that she wanted to curl around it until it's all inside of her.

I wondered if there was yet something else I did not know that could cause sex to be even more messy. Well, indeed there was and for Angie it was just another part of her, her naturalness, her liquidity. I felt dirty but she didn't, I felt unsure in her confidence, but with her saying it felt best really around the same time each month and finding some tissues in her twisted up pants to end the matter softly as she reached up to touch my ear, then near my lips. I felt her nails trace up the back of my neck, a path miles long that seemed to just go on and on until I was dizzy for it. Her happiness became essential to my own.

"That felt different that time Earl, like something happened."

"A'course something happened Angie."

"No, I mean different than just that. I don't know, felt like something. Something special between us."

❧   ❧   ❧

"SOMETIMES WHEN I was sad I cried to myself," Angie told me, "and I wished I had a twin sister. The boy next door would hit me, and I'd hit him back and I'd tell my mom and she'd just only say 'be nice.' That's when I knew I wanted more boyfriends and fewer husbands."

We were alone, snuck off in the daytime into the woods. Being out there without darkness as a blanket was electricity between us.

"We'll whisper to make it more romantic," said Angie. "Now Earl, let me see it."

"No, it's embarrassing," I answered her, looking away like something so fascinating was over there, I wanted her to look too.

"Over here, Earl. Now, c'mon, you're willing to put it in me, so at least let me see it up close."

Most Reeve girls had learned somewhere that they were supposed to at least pretend it was embarrassing, 'cause it was over quicker usually I guess, like getting something done, eating when you're really hungry and not tasting the food.

"I like the top here, right here, this mushroom part. Soft, like a rose petal. What's that feel like when I touch there?"

Well, it felt goddamn amazing, and I shiver a bit to recall it now on this bus in front of people, what, some forty years later? That's a long time for a feeling to last.

"Now you look at me," Angie said, smiling with a secret. I was feeling the sweat start around the edges of my hair when she pressed my head into a place I am pretty sure the last time I had been they said "it's a boy, ma'am" to my mom.

I might as well have journeyed to Mars, as it would have seemed more familiar. After seventeen years of imagining it, then thinking about it, then poking into it, here she was. It is easy now to forget that in 1977 there was no Internet porn, no magazines that you could get in Reeve, at least, showing such things, and even the human biology book with the drawings in it was on the restricted shelf at school and you needed Mrs. Coughlin's permission, which would be like asking Muley to see his mom naked. Actually, that'd be less embarrassing.

"So now you're gonna kiss me down there Earl. It's only fair, give and take, you know."

This I thought I knew about. Muley had told us, having learned the mysteries of such things from an older brother who had been in the Marine Corps in Japan and thus knew. We didn't believe him, like we didn't believe him when he said people there ate uncooked sushi fish. Why would anyone do that? It made no sense.

Angie was pretty insistent, I guess having learned something about these kinds of things herself from a source more reliable than Muley's older brother in the Marines. She held my head and kind of directed me. Pink, soft, a little bitter, maybe astringent after I learned that word, oh, wetter now, starting to understand, faster, faster, no no, slower now, there, right there, easy now, put your tongue right there, there oh, oh oh—

Oh.

"Did I hurt you Angie?"

"No, no Earl. Shhh now, no more talking."

I understood fully why people would do that.

Angie got to use her dead dad's old work car all the time. Her mom worked of course, but her being a widow, she also felt that desperate loneliness that pulled at her. She took up with a man from Monroe that involved her spending much time out of the house. So me and Angie would drive around, talking, listening to the radio. She kept liking to ask me what I was gonna do next. I thought I knew the answer and even trying to show off a bit, would tell her how expensive college was, and how pointless it was, and talked up the job at the factory I believed I would be starting the week after graduation. Hourly wage, health plan (whatever that was), retirement plan (whatever that was, we were seventeen years old) and paid holidays. Against the required calculus class and Freshman Writing Workshop Ohio State was going to make her get through, my job prospects seemed attractive, but to her college was gonna be about expanding her boundaries, whatever that was, maybe even dating a colored guy, she said while we were driving.

"What about running away?" she asked. "We got a tank of gas and my mom don't care if I'm home or not. We could drive somewhere, right now, go to Pittsburgh or New York. It'd be just us Earl, we'd get an apartment and we'd cook together and find jobs and we could sleep together in a bed every night. What do you say?"

I probably was thinking more about the together in a bed part than anything else, but I reached over, turned the radio up and pushed my foot past hers to kick the accelerator closer to the floor. "Let's drive," I shouted, and I leaned out the window so I could feel the wind wash Reeve off of me. We pretended we had a top to put down, and as we crossed the Reeve city line Angie leaned way out her side, hair flying behind her like a kite tail, and shouted "Fuuuuuuuuuuuuuuuck YOOOOOOOOOOOOOU I ain't never comin' baaaaaaaaaaaaaaaaaaaaaaack!"

We drove that car way too fast, and it was only a couple of hours when we had to stop for more gas, at a highway place along Interstate 70 halfway into Pennsylvania. Even being in another state felt sexy and tingly and exotic.

"Let's pretend we're married," she said, laughing as we went into the service plaza fast-food place to see we were the youngest there by two or three lifetimes. "Gimme your jacket over my shoulders."

"Honey, did you remember the milk?"

"Oh no dear, sorry. I thought I'd get it after my bowling night."

"What time is the mortgage due, dearest love?"

"Perhaps, my darling, we should travel again soon."

"Oh sweetheart, darling, I love it when you take me out!"

Starting a life-changing adventure spontaneously with only $27 in loose bills is not necessarily the smartest plan. Filling up burned through half of that money and after two burgers and some Dr. Peppers, me and Angie were sitting too quietly.

"Maybe we should head back now," I told her. "This was fun and all, but my folks'll be expecting me before midnight or I'll get grounded and I got football practice starting soon."

"What're you talking about? New York's still hours away. We're gonna have to drive all night just to get there by sunrise. I wanna see the sun come up there."

"You're serious about this? C'mon, like when you tried to convince me you got a real tattoo, it was all fun playing at it, but when it got boring you just wiped it away with spit. Let's go home."

"Earl, I'm going. I meant it, and I meant for you to come along. Nothing to go back to in Reeve."

"Your mom—"

"My mom won't be home for days and until she gets around to doing laundry and don't see my clothes in the hamper, probably won't even notice me gone. Kids run away all the time, it ain't that big a deal. You ain't gonna learn nothing more in high school anyway, and then what, work in that factory? That what you living for, to turn into your dad? You wanna marry me, get drunk on Saturday, slap me around a little and throw me on the bed before you pass out sweaty on top of me? Hell Earl, even that ain't likely. The factory laid off men for the first time ever, and when James got Evelyn pregnant and went for his job, he only got one 'cause his daddy begged the foreman. You wanna die in Reeve alongside the whole goddamn town? This is about doing something, getting off your ass, saying something, seeing what a shitty place this is and what a jam place we could move to. I don't want to be living in Reeve at age sixty in my mom's house with her books and cats. Let's go."

"Angie, I thought you were kidding about New York, like you do. I'm seventeen. My mom still makes my bed. What I gave you for gas was allowance money. I ain't never been more than five miles from Reeve alone before. I can't live in New York, get a job, or move in with you. I mean, I'm on the football team."

"Let's go."

The words hung up high enough that I couldn't reach them.

"I can't."

It sounded like a fight, but a fight was where one side is trying to win over the other. Sitting there alongside Interstate 70, we were just saying goodbye in a really crummy way. I know now that I simply did not know how to love her. Interstate 70 runs practically anywhere. But not me, not that night. I was scared and I had too much of the small town in me. I didn't see—couldn't see—that the road went both ways. Angie did kiss me, did thank me for the gas money, and made me again scribble down my address so she could write from New York. She took my jacket off her shoulders and folded it, handing it back to me. I stood alone in that fast-food parking lot, and I watched the tail lights of her car merge into traffic, into the night, the wind, the new rain until I could not distinguish her ride from any of the others heading away. It was chilly, and I unfolded my jacket, smelling the last of her fade off as the wind came up and took even that from me. I struggled with women for a long time, trying out different things, learning to repeat things I read in Hallmark cards to make them feel I cared, often to good results. But it was hard, and I could remember when, once, it had been effortless.

Angie wrote me a postcard like I heard tourists buy ten for a dollar in Times Square that said GREETINGS FROM NEW YORK, but I otherwise never heard from her again. Kept the postcard though, for a long time, kept that instead of her, I guess. There were never two days in a row that I did not think of her, never a time when I watched cars on a highway that I didn't wonder why I didn't have the courage for Angie.

Hitchhiking back to Reeve took less time than I worried it might. First trucker refused to take me, pointing to a sticker on his cab that said NO RIDERS, NO EXCEPTIONS. I asked him which was more important, a person or a sticker and he kinda laughed, kinda didn't, said he had a wife and kids and drew a circle in the dust around the NO EXCEPTIONS line. I had better luck later and made it home. My old man grounded me even though Mom said she was just glad I was safe after doing something so stupid.

Summer Storms

WE STARTED OUT like we often did, jumping the fence and climbing up one of Reeve's two water towers. Me, Muley, Tim and Rich were always together that summer, always had been together since whenever. We were on the football team together, and we planned one more big night out before training started. The ladder up the water tower had sort of a cage around it, but it was old and rusty even then and you had to wonder each time if you'd be the one in the newspaper story about the dumb teenager killed climbing the water tower. Evening was creeping as delicately as that new kid on the first day of school. We fought over who'd climb up first, 'cause the first guy didn't get his fingers stepped on like the trailing three, and I won. First up was best too because you'd look up that ladder and the light would fade off into the dark a couple of yards ahead of you. You'd look up and see nothing but night and you were flying.

Up top was a walkway with a railing you never felt right leaning against. Muley grabbed my belt and shoved me at the same time, pulling me back of course even as I saw all the way down just for a second. It was an old trick for us but it made my balls tingle every time. A bunch of kids had spray-painted their names, their graduation years and their favorite bands up there, but that was little kids' stuff. For us, standing there with all of Reeve unfolded below, that was the prize. You could see the factory, giving off an orange glow, the dark streak where the river was, see cars moving along like Matchbox toys. Little kids would say, "There's my house," the first time up, but that was only for first-timers. Each of us was quiet, tracing streets we knew, picking out our last girlfriend's house and wondering if she was home, and of course looking down at the high school and that football field where we'd sweat and suffer over the last few weeks of August for Coach. We're all always somewhere, but this made our connection to the place real. We were not a group prone to talking about beauty and art and that kind of stuff, but that view from up there was beautiful. Every one of us imagined flying off the walkway and sailing over Reeve and that wasn't a little kid thing to think. Up there that night, measuring the awesomeness, everything was still ahead of us, anything seemed possible to us.

"Hey Earl, you believe in Heaven?"

"What Muley, you drunk already man?"

"No, it's just up here, I don't know, I start to think about those kind of things."

"I guess so. My old man's always talking about going to Hell, so I guess that means there's Heaven, too."

"Why don't you two go hug under a rainbow and write a fucking poem or something?"

"Seriously guys, I been to Heaven. Her name was Patty Kennedy."

"And if she blew you that must've been a living Hell for her."

"What if every time you said something that stupid God made your wiener one inch shorter?"

"Shut up, this is serious."

"Muley's would be like only that long."

"No you guys, seriously, do you think we're going to Heaven?"

"Shit, Muley, now you got me thinking about it."

"So whatta you think?"

"I think so. Whatever we done wrong, it ain't been nothing so bad, just screwing around stuff. We ain't never killed anybody or nothing."

"I heard Earl's dad tell someone to go to Hell. Wouldn't it be cool if you do that, like it was a God kinda secret that if you said it, then it happened to the person you said it to."

"The way Earl's old man cusses, Hell'd be full already."

"I had this dream once where I was a girl."

"Me too, but I had to go to school naked."

"You guys are stupid, remembering things that never happened."

"So what about this then. What if we inherited sins, like from our dads?"

"Isn't that what Jesus fixed?"

"What's your problem? Did your mom smoke during pregnancy or somethin'?"

"Man, we'd better check because that's important."

"So we'd go to Heaven then right, 'cept maybe Earl's dad?"

"Shut up you guys, and be serious. Lookit out there, how pretty. That'd be what Heaven looks like."

"Do they have night in Heaven? I thought it was always daytime, because it was above the clouds and all."

"You guys are idiots. We better climb down before we get caught up here and for sure we'd end up in Hell."

We moved on to Muley's back shed, where his old man kept a steel bass boat. The shed was a pretty special place for us, smelling like old, wet sweaters and full of cobwebs and stuff like car parts and ratty sports gear that was as attractive then as free beer is now. There was an old Coke sign with a girl in a thick 1950s bikini that provided most of us our first unrequited but warming mental image. We all remembered how cool it stayed in there on hot days, and how we could warm it up with the electric heater in the winter and make it smell like burnt toast. The bass boat held a place of pride among the junk, but had seen better days. We tried to fix it with Bondo, the putty stuff you use on car dents, but that didn't stick too well to all the rust, and the thing floated more out of stubbornness than anything else. Flat bottom, seats two safely. Rides low in the water, and you got to paddle. We'd take it out on the river from time to time, drinking beer when we could, horsing around when we couldn't.

This night we did have some beer and the four of us decided it made a lot of sense to take the boat out on the river after dark, kind of a thrill. It was a warm, heavy, humid night, still then soft around us. The moon was hanging. I don't know what you call it, but it looked like God's toenail up there. A riot of stars you could only see after your eyes got used to it. Lightning bugs. Car sounds far off on the highway. The current was light and the river half dry in summer, so we figured loading the four of us into a boat made for two wouldn't be a problem. Then we met Pam, this girl Tim sort of liked and Tim made us take her along too. Pam had been the third girl in our grade to start wearing a bra, and Tim had it on good authority she had lost her virginity already and was willing to lose it some more. She had a Farrah 'do. We all had that poster on our walls, if not on our minds, that summer, so that was important.

Things started out okay, as okay as four drunk teenage boys with a boat and beer sniffing after one nervous teenage girl can be. Our enthusiasm was fuel. We got the boat into the water and climbed in well enough. Muley had the idea of tying a rope through the plastic rings on the six packs of Genesee so we could tow them along behind us and they'd stay cold. Tim devoted himself to bossing us around to make himself look like a big guy, and Pam devoted herself to worrying about five people in a boat that might safely hold two.

Pam was right like girls then usually were about those kind of things. The boat drifted along with the current, ending up in the center of the river two beers later. We could see a few lights reflecting off the water, and it was kinda pretty. I guess that is what inspired Tim to try and put his arm around Pam, who was less inspired by the romantic scene and shrugged him off a bit too hard. The boat rocked and water came over the shallow sides. I was laughing, and so was Muley, who started rocking the boat even more, when the whole thing flipped over. The five of us were dumped into the river. It wasn't too deep; I couldn't touch the bottom, but it was easy enough to doggy paddle over to the far bank. I wasn't even breathing too hard, and looked over, laughing, at Tim, Rich and a really unhappy Pam. Her Farrah 'do was ruined. The boat was gone.

"Where's Muley?"

"I don't know, maybe over there?"

No Muley.

Tim and Pam went off looking for him down the river bank, thinking maybe he swam off that way. Rich heard him first— Muley, in the water, shouting for us. I figured he was kidding around like always, pretending to drown in eight feet of warm water, when I saw Rich dive back in. I went in right after him, and we reached Muley in a few wet splashes. Rich grabbed him first, and we pulled him over to the bank. He was crying, snot all down his face, white as Wonder Bread. He had been wearing his heavy work boots, lace-ups, and they had filled with water, pulling him under. Muley was a strong kid back then, and was able to claw his way up to the surface and shout, but if Rich had not gone in after him, he'd a' drowned that night in the river while we watched.

It was either Muley's earlier laughing or Muley's recent shouting that brought out the cops. Someone must have heard it all and called them. The one fat cop came up to me and said, "Son, how many kids were in that boat?" And I said, truthfully, "Sir, there were five of us." Me, Muley and Rich were right there. Tim and Pam hadn't come back, likely seeing the cop car lights and running. Five of us, just like I said.

"Don't worry son, we'll find your friends." The cop put me in the back of his car with a blanket and waded into the river. Three other cops pulled up and went right in, too, and right after that the fire truck came with the siren going and all those men waded into the river. Flashlights were swinging criss-cross over the water and the cops would yell for a bit, then tell each other to "Be quiet and just listen for a minute goddammit, there's two kids out there somewhere. There was five of 'em in that boat when it flipped, and we only got three on the bank! We ain't gonna let them other two missing die for no reason—"

I figured out the reason. The next time the fat cop came over panting and tomato-faced to see how I was doing, I told him that Tim and Pam probably weren't coming back. He put his hand on my shoulder and said something about, "Not if I can help it, son." This time, before he turned back, I told him Tim and Pam weren't in the river. Nobody drowned. Nobody was missing. Tim and Pam had just run away. When he asked me how many in the boat, I didn't want to lie and so I said, "Five officer, honest. Maybe you misunderstood me?"

For some reason then the fat cop got angry with me, using cuss words and all. Me, Muley and Rich ended up having to call our parents from the police station, and later they had to pay a fine for us endangering a law enforcement official and wasting emergency resources such as the fire truck and flashlights. That cost me most of my summer allowance money and my dad was pissed. Muley's dad screamed at him for twenty minutes after Johnny Carson was over that night, and swatted his ass for the first time since fifth grade. Rich got off easy, but his old man was upset, saying that if Rich had drowned, or had been arrested for real, there'd go his senior year on the football team and there'd go any chance of playing ball at some college, why'd he think he could throw away his life like that? Tim never got to make out with Pam that night, but they didn't go to jail either and he walked her home and she said maybe she'd think about it. It was the first time I realized you could die without getting old first, and that stuck with me.

WE LOVED FOOTBALL because we had grown up loving football. Muley, me, and most of my friends, including Tim and Rich, played football. Our town had two teams, our team and some other kids who sort of made a team from the parochial school, but they only played against other kids in the God league. We played for Reeve, and in Reeve that was close to being with God. We played in the Southwestern Conference against other towns and then when we were winners we'd play in Regionals and up to, maybe in the year of 1977, State Championships. Everyone knew the year before Rob had gone on to actual tryouts at Ohio State, and in the past the Bernard boys had both made the team at OSU, even if they did not play much in the one game we saw on television each Thanksgiving weekend.

Muley was thinking back to football training camp, and said to me:

I remember Coach's whistle, how it sounded bigger and louder in the locker room than outside, sort of telling you in there Coach Polanski was what mattered. He'd wait for us to start peeling off the sweaty gear and then gather us around him. He'd say things like, "Alright. I know it's late and you all want to get outta here, but lemme say something about today's practice. I think you all let your dicks hang out too much this summer. You better shape up, boys, or we're all in for some long practices. Hell, I find chunks of better men in my shit every morning."

Old man Polanski didn't want us to let down Reeve, and Reeve loved him back for it. He was officially a teacher at the high school, History of Our United States, which was only about from Columbus to the Civil War, even though the textbook went up to the Korean War. Everyone on the football team got an A from him except Ron Curry, who he thought wasn't pulling his weight. Coach was stuck, 'cause the school board made it a rule that anyone who showed up every day for practice could be on the team, so we wasn't violating laws made by sissies who probably never even played the game themselves. Back in our dads' day, not just anyone got on the team. It was called Judgment Day, when everyone was gathered on the field at the end of summer and Coach called out names. Winners forward, losers to the locker rooms, and fuck you and your life in Reeve if you were on the wrong side of the line. Different now, sort of.

"Who're you, boy?" said Coach.

"I'm Andrew, sir. Freshman."

"You call my dad 'Sir.' You better learn quick to call me Coach."

"Yes sir."

"Andrew, you big enough to play football? How the hell tall are you anyway?"

"I'm five foot three, Coach."

"Five foot three. Who knew they could stack shit that high in Reeve?"

We all laughed as Coach looked around the room for our reaction. Coach was always kidding like that, making the new guys feel noticed and welcoming them and all.

"And for you knuckleheads with concussions, get your underwear on right. Yellow stains in the front and brown stains in the back."

Coach was kind of a role model for us.

"Now, I heard some of you like to do some drinking."

Coach, high on the smell of his own piss, often gave us advice to develop us as adult men.

"And I can't say that's all bad, but what I'm talking about is the fighting you boys seem to do after that. I don't want none of you to get hurt in some silly-ass bar fight. We are here to play football, to win for Reeve, not get into fights."

We had heard this one before. Here came the best part every year:

"However, if you are gonna fight, you might as well kick the shit outta the other guy, or you're gonna have to answer to me. We beat 'em on the field and we beat 'em off the field. We are winners, don't leave here forgetting that. Now get."

Him leaving the locker room meant we were going to initiate the new guys. Just anyone could join the team because of that dumb rule, but it was us that made it so you had to prove you were good enough. That was initiation. Coaches had their office attached to the locker room and could hear everything. You cussed one of them, even quietly, and he'd be in your face in a flash second, moving out of that office like you never seen a fat man move, sometimes still with a pint bottle of rotgut in one hand and a cigarette dropping ash in the other. But somehow they never heard anything when it was initiation. Once they signaled they didn't care, it put the bullies in charge.

We started out making the freshmen sing, sometimes funny songs, sometimes something from the radio, and sometimes we'd make 'em pair off and sing love songs out loud to each other. Nothing funnier than some scared kid singing some romantic Elton John song to another guy, especially since we made them do it. If they didn't, they'd get a load of muscle ache cream in their jock, burn the hell outta their balls because it was greasy and didn't wash off. I got it my freshman year and it didn't dry all through practice, but I sat in a cold bath tub for two hours when I got home. I told Mom I was relaxing, and she assumed I was beatin' off, but Dad knew, and stuck his head in to laugh at me like he got laughed at a hundred years ago when seniors did it to him. It was tradition, and that mattered for us. Nobody got hurt really, just singing and stuff really. I doubt half of them even remember what happened.

Ron Curry was not a freshman but a senior like us, and so officially he was not supposed to be initiated. I don't know why we hated him, but Coach did and so we did. Maybe we just had to hate someone 'cause I guess it made us feel stronger to hack at someone like him. Ron was fat and pasty, that kinda kid who'd never tan no matter what, so Coach called him Snowball, and so did we. Even though he was a senior we made him sing too, and one time we made him bend over the tackling dummy and hump it in front of everybody. He sang "I'm in the Mood for Love" so many times in that locker room that we stopped telling him to do it and he just did it whenever we pulled him into the center. In the beginning, he cried like a pussy, and once he cried in the cafeteria when we threw mashed potatoes at him because he wore a new shirt we didn't like 'cause it was sort of girly, but mostly he just did it. He never had a girlfriend, of course, right? His dad we heard made him go out for the football team each year to make a man outta him, even though he did not want to, so maybe givin' in to us wasn't so different than givin' in to his dad. Did you know he was the only guy from that year moved out of Reeve right after graduation? All along we knew he wasn't part of the team.

Ron was always on the second string defense, them kids who stood in for the other team to let our offense practice. Coach called them cannon fodder, a word we did not understand, but must have had something to do with the Civil War 'cause Coach was that teacher.

This one time, he told Ron to rush in at the quarterback, blitz the hell out of him, and then he quietly told the offense to expect it and cream Ron's ass as a kind of joke. Well, the ball was snapped, and Ron ran ahead just like he was told, saw them big guys laying for him, and backed up, as he was a fool but he wasn't stupid. Coach was pissed, blowing his whistle and kicking up dirt. He grabbed Ron by the face mask so that he could jerk his head around like punctuation while he chewed him out. "Goddammit, you do what I tell you," Coach screamed, them veins in his neck even sticking out. "This is not a democracy, you ain't got a choice, you do what you are told to do." Spit was flying, and Ron couldn't back up because Coach had him by the mask. Coach ended by telling him that on the next play he goddamn better rush and blitz like he was told. So the ball was snapped and Ron started in, seeing the guys laying for him, and kept rushing forward 'cause there was nothing he could do but take the hit.

We had this thing called two-on-one drills. One guy would get the ball and have to run straight into two other guys just in front of him. They were supposed to try and knock the ball loose, make you fumble it, which was the point of the drill. It was rough, especially when you were the smaller part of the triangle, or when the other two knew each other and set up to hit one high and one low. But you did it to toughen up. Coach set Ron up again, handing him the ball with two big seniors in front. Ron ran like he was supposed to, and they knocked the ball loose. Usually then Coach would cuss you and call the next three. But that time with Ron, he blew his whistle and said, "Run it again, same boys." Ron lost the ball. Run it again. Again. And again until on the fifth try Ron didn't get back up. He just laid on the ground, I think the wind knocked outta him or something. Coach stood over him, yelling to get up and run it again. "Get up or I'll fuckin' throw your fairy ass off this team." I think Ron was even crying by this time. We all just stood around in a circle. I guess we could have helped him up or something, but we were scared and it really wasn't any of our business, right? But man, old Ron caught his breath and we all heard him: "You can't throw me off the team. And I can't quit. But I won't get up." It was all quiet, and nobody expected Coach to say nothing and just walk off, leaving Ron there, but that's what he did.

Coaches worked hard to make us winners, and they tolerated nothing from us when we didn't pull our weight. Polanski would stand on the blocking sled drinking pop, making it that much heavier when we had to push it across the field. Seeing him drinking that cold pop when we weren't allowed to have water made us angry and, he said, meaner for the game. I can remember the water condensing on the outside of that bottle, every drop and detail. I would have begged, I would have twisted Ron Curry's arm off, to lick some of that cold water from that bottle on those August days. But Coach would take a long pull just to piss us off and say, "You haven't earned your drink." And we'd push him across the dry grass and eat dust until we knew we'd at least earned his respect. It was a good thing, though we hated it while we were there. "You play how you practice," he said, "and you live the way you play the game. Yesterday's touchdowns don't win tomorrow's game."

Most mistakes got you push-ups or laps around the field. The worst screw-ups and Assistant Coach O'Brian took you out behind the stands to "move the hole." He had a hole dug in the hard clay near one end of the bleachers, and then he'd mark the ground somewhere further away. You'd get a shovel, walk to the mark, pick up a load of dirt and carry it to the hole. Throw it in. Do that enough times and the old hole would get filled and a new hole would be where you did the digging. You moved the hole. O'Brian, if he liked you, would make the two holes only a couple of yards apart, and if he really liked you he'd put one of them by the fence, where the water pipe had broken two summers ago and the earth was still soft. But if he was mad at you, like you missed a tackle or forgot your gear, man, he'd put those holes in the sun at opposite ends of the bleachers and you'd be out there all afternoon sweating blood. O'Brian said a lot of men were created in those yards between the two holes, and we believed that. I never knew what happened to that guy.

Coach Polanski had his heart attack right there on the field that one game like everyone knows, but O'Brian just disappeared.

GUYS LIKE MULEY never saw through it. Man, even now he didn't see how they failed us. We wanted those men, Polanski and O'Brian and the others, to be our heroes. We all knew our dads too well, saw their flaws, watched them fight with our moms, watched them get told what to do at work, watched them beg for a broom to stand up with after their trained work left Reeve for some China guy who would do it for a few cents an hour so that everyone in America could afford a big-screen TV; even Dad bought a forty-two incher for the Super Bowl one year. But we came to know that Polanski and the other coaches weren't nothing more than anyone else, they were just high school teachers in a small town, and not even good teachers. People like Muley still buy into the myth, still want to think of 'em as legends, talk about football, march in the Memorial Day parades and say God bless.

We were meant to be unhappy. Lose your job to an Asian sweat shop, but think you're ahead because prices come down, all's well until next month when bigger and better is on sale. I bought a cell phone and one week later got a letter from the company about upgrading to a newer model. You're not pretty enough (buy makeup), you don't smell right (deodorant to smell less, perfume to smell more), your car, your house, your electronics, your porch, your boat, your RV, your dick are all too small. Work hard and you'll get what you want, people say, but in some impatient reality you're just chasing things. It's the

hoping to kill myself. Instead, my old man made me puke them up then beat the shit outta me. Well, you go to Hell man. I wish they'd broken your arms that day in the shower, your neck too. Okay Dad, I got on the bus with him, like you said. Can I get off now?"

Ron was talking about my last day of football ever. We were all in the shower, one big tiled room with shower heads all around. We were tan from the summer, white butts and brown backs. Soap came in bars, good for washing and better for throwing at each other. Once that started, everybody went at it, some aiming high for a bloody nose shot and others looking to whack you in the nuts. A good shot to the nads could bring a guy down, and one time Tim even puked a little, he caught it so hard. He fell down and everybody turned and threw soap at him on the floor, even me and Muley. That was hilarious and we still talk about it, even on this bus years later.

Then that day took a bad turn. I was givin' and getting in about equal portions when I slipped. I hit the floor in a funny way, sort of ankle first somehow, and for a second everything went white. I must have shouted and cursed, but between the water runnin' and everybody yelling, even I didn't hear myself. Some, then all, the boys saw me down and chucked soap at me. At some point my yelling must have got loud enough, 'cause they stopped and somebody called for Coach Polanski. Everyone kind of backed off, lining the walls and shutting down most of the showers while I just laid there. I once sliced off a chunk of my hand trying to open a paint can with a wood chisel instead of a screwdriver, and that was a kind of slow-motion pain, taking a moment or two as I watched the blood pool out before it hurt. This one was some hot thing starting in my ankle but feeling more like it came from deeper inside me, an everywhere kind of pain. Polanski, fully dressed, felt my ankle and said out loud that something might be sprained bad and for one of the guys to call a doctor. He chased the boys out of the shower while they was still all wet, and the last thing I remember lying there on the shower floor was him walking over in his special coach shoes to a dripping faucet, rubber soles squeaking on the wet floor, and him shutting the water off.

When I got dropped off from the doctor in front of my house, my dog came running out. Dad said he could never figure out the point of cats, so we didn't have one. I had had the dog, however, for a long time, changing its name from stupid kid stuff like Hot Wheels and Spider Man to what I thought was cooler names such as Thor or Killer, but the rhythms between us had been set for so long that she'd answer to just about anything out of my mouth. Even so, when I came home with my ankle still half-wrapped in tape she approached me with some caution, kinda working her way toward me instead of running straight out the door. She pulled up short and sniffed at me, almost like I was different. Must've been the smell of the athletic tape; dogs are sensitive to change.

Inside, the TV was on without nobody in the living room when Dad came in from work. I had gone up to my room for the bed, and was watching the old black-and-white, the picture making my room all blue that late in the afternoon. I heard Mom send Dad upstairs without him even washing up, a big deal in my house.

"Your mother told me you hurt yourself in practice today. Hurt bad?" I had started to pull the tape off because it itched. Dad looked at my ankle, kind of touching it around the sides like he was checking tomatoes at a roadside stand. He saw the black and blue marks up my leg from where the soap bars hit, and poked at them a little with that crooked finger with the top missing. It was kind of creepy, like I was imagining it burned or something wherever he pressed, but truth, I didn't feel nothing.

"Naw. It don't hurt too bad. Itches a little 'cause of the tape."

"That's my boy."

He left. Down to the kitchen for a beer. I wasn't supposed to, but I could hear him and Mom in the kitchen through the open heating grates. You could look right through them, too, they was just a hole really for the hot air to rise through. No blowers then.

"He don't look bad," said my old man.

"Doctor said he could start moving around by tomorrow if it don't hurt him. Just a nasty sprain. It ain't too bad considering."

"That's good."

"Doctor also said no more football this year. Can't chance hurtin' it again for a while."

"That's too bad Sissy."

"I know you didn't want the boy to go away next year, but you could at least—"

"I don't need to hear it. He wasn't good enough anyway. Let him work for a while, better for him."

Mom backed down like she always did. I heard Dad pull open the refrigerator before Mom spoke again.

"Don't touch that food. It's for the party tomorrow."

"What party?"

"With Stan and Lori. You known for a week."

"I ain't in the mood for a party. Me and Stan had some words. Anyway, I thought you'd cancel it now on account of Earl messing up his ankle."

"What for? He's gonna be up and around by morning."

"Well, you might think of another reason, 'cause we ain't gonna have no party here. I'm gonna go watch TV." And I heard him go off to the living room as Mom shouted after him. He was never a warm or happy man for sure, but alcohol frayed whatever leash he kept on himself.

Mom was talking past loud at him across the house. "We're gonna have the party tomorrow night. I want to have it. We're gonna have it Ray, and you're gonna be there. I don't give a shit if you and Stan ain't getting along 'cause this ain't for you two anyway."

I was sick of hearing them fight, and I yelled down the grate to Mom to be quiet, that I was trying to sleep. I heard her throw something in the garbage as Dad turned up the sound on the TV, and I put the pillow over my head to make it all go away.

MY MOM WAS on the bus. I think she can hear me think, or maybe I'm talking out loud, and she knew I lied to her about wanting to go to sleep that day to make her be quiet. Mom said:

I wanted that party. Even though we was just having Stan and Lori over to play cards, I wanted to do it, and I called it a party because I wanted to think of it that way. Even at work I was excited. The girls that waited tables after school started checking in to work, and I got all huffy at them for keeping me from punching out until that clock had clicked over to 4:31. I was even intent on making up a bit with your dad. He worked hard, and the changes at the factory were tough on him, so I timed it just right to run into him just as we were both coming back to the house. We had fought a lot those days, and if you wanted to keep on the bright side, it did give us both some practice in making up and putting on best behavior.

"How's Earl doin'?" your father asked me.

"I called home this afternoon, and Earl's already making plans for tomorrow night. He's almost his old surly self again."

"What're we having for dinner?"

"I don't know, I hate to mess up the kitchen with Stan and Lori comin' over soon."

"Maybe we should go to Dairy Queen or something," your dad suggested. His best behavior.

"Earl!," I shouted to you, "Hobble yourself down here. We're going to the Dairy Queen for hamburgers and ice cream. And no excuses, we are going as a family!"

Then I knew your dad was sorry for the other night, 'cause he said:

"Earl, you heard your mother. Get moving."

"You talk to Stan yet, Ray? Try and patch up whatever is buggin' you two?"

"No, not really. We was busy."

"Well, that'll just give you more to talk about tonight. I gotta get some makeup on."

Things went well at the Dairy Queen.

"Now Stan and Lori is coming in about an hour, so we can't take too long. Grab that ice cream, we'll keep it in the ice-box at home and eat it later. You can have it Earl, cheer you up. Earl's staying home one more night to recuperate."

"Is that right? You made that decision by yourself, did you Earl?" said Dad.

Later, from up in my room I heard it all. Doorbell ringing. Mom flipping on the porch light.

"Stan."

"Ray."

"Well, I'm glad we could make it," said Lori.

"Uh-huh," added Stan as if Lori had pulled a string back of his neck.

Mom was still trying. "So why don't you all have a seat here with Ray, and I'll go get us something to eat?"

"Here, let me give you a hand," said Lori in the kitchen. "Sissy, we almost didn't make it here tonight. I think something bad happened between Stan and Ray. I had to practically drag Stan over here."

"What went on? Ray's been in an odd mood."

"Stan won't tell me. Says it's some kind of man-to-man thing."

"Well, we girls'll just have to have a good time in spite of them. C'mon Lori, we're still friends."

I heard them move to the living room. The TV was on.

"Here's the food."

"It looks good, honey," said Stan.

"Well don't tell me, tell Sissy. She made it."

"How's Rob doing?" Mom was still pitching, still hoping for a nice evening together.

"He's fine. Won his softball game last night. Factory team isn't too bad this year."

The long pauses were filled with TV noise. Mom usually hated having it on when people were over, but I think this night she let it go on purpose.

"Uh, I heard about Earl," Stan said, testing the waters with Dad. "He feelin' any better?"

Dad looked at Mom, who really looked back at Dad.

"Yeah. He'll be good as before by tomorrow. Ain't really hurt bad at all."

"He gonna be able to get back to practice soon?"

Mom stepped in between their conversation. "Doctor said no. He said Earl shouldn't risk gettin' hurt again. He's done this year."

"Boy taking it hard, I suspect?"

"Uh-huh."

"Well, the card table is all set up," I could hear Mom say. There were card shuffling noises, and it sounded like they were playing more or less quietly for a while. She and Dad were partners at the table and usually enjoyed this. I was kinda rooting for Mom.

"Excuse me for a second, gotta take a leak," Dad said, and I heard him walk to the toilet room. The small talk once he was gone boosted Mom's spirits a little, I could tell, just by listening to her. She talked one way around Dad, choosing words slowly, like she was thinking more than she was doing now with just friends. She was happy and even suggested they switch up, with her and Stan playing partners across the table while Lori waited for Dad to come back.

After the toilet door closed and he came back, that all quiet time lasted only a little while longer until I heard Dad make that sound, sucking in air, like he did when he was starting to get up a head of steam over something.

"What's the matter?" Dad said.

"Nothing." Stan was buying time, sorting out that fight-or-flight question.

"No, you acted like something was wrong. What is it?" He was challenging now. Mom knew this sound, too much beer mixed with something acid-like that was always waiting inside him.

"Ray, please," she said.

"What's eating you Stan?" It was like a summer storm gathering. It was gonna rain, just not sure exactly when, but soon enough that you started heading for the car.

"Ain't nothing eating me. I just didn't like how Sissy played that last card, that's all."

"No, wait a minute. You can't act rude, 'specially to my wife. She's your partner here, mister, in my house."

"Ray, c'mon, let's just play cards." Mom tried to head it off, but the first rain drops were hitting the ground, big and heavy, puffing up the dust.

"I don't have people over to be insulting to my wife."

"I didn't insult nobody," Stan said.

"Stan, why don't you let it go?" Lori was pleading now, talking to Stan but chances were she was looking at Mom while she said it.

"Don't tell me what to do."

"I'm not trying to tell you what to do, honey. I just think—"

"Lori, maybe we should serve the cake now." Mom trying one more diversion. Cake sometimes worked.

"Maybe we don't want none of your cake," Stan snapped, and that was it. The clouds opened and the rain started not sweet, but with purpose.

"You watch how you're talkin'," Dad said to Stan.

"You don't tell me what to do neither." Stan stood up. Thunder crack.

"C'mon Stan, maybe we should get on home. It's getting late."

"Yeah, maybe it is," snapped Dad.

Just 9:30. I had a clock you could see in the dark.

"Thanks for the snacks Sissy," said Lori. Her voice changed to a whisper. "I'll call you, okay?"

"Aw Stan—Lori. Now can't you stay just a few more minutes? I've got some nice cake."

"We should get going," said Lori. "I'll call you."

That screen door shut hard. TV was back to too loud.

"Where're you going with that cake, Sissy?"

"I'm bringing it up to Earl to see if he wants any. Ain't nobody eatin' it down here. Can't go to waste."

I hated when they fought and I wanted nothing to do with it. I knew Mom was upset, but I did not want any cake.

"What?"

"I brought you a piece of cake."

"No thanks. I still gotta stay in shape, in case I can go back to practice."

"Well, I'll just leave it on the nightstand. Did you see? Your dad had me looking in the garage for things to sell off at another yard sale, and I found a box of your old blocks, from when you was little. I brought them up with me in case you wanna see them."

I remembered those blocks. They were one of my favorite toys, even as I got older. Made of wood, all the edges were worn round from being handled over and over. I built forts and firehouses, even what I thought was a pretty good replica of the factory once out of them. I'd build something and then call Mom to look. She'd be all smiling, trying to guess what it was so's not to hurt my feelings. As I got older, I figured out that game and would just tell her, "It's a spaceship."

I was reaching for the box, you know, just to see, not that I wanted to play with them anymore, when Mom said:

"We might be able to figure something out, you know."

"What're you talking about?"

"About college and all."

"Ain't no scholarship coming." I pointed at my ankle with the cake fork. I'd decided to have just a little taste after all. I knew I wasn't going back.

"I know that. I was thinking about something else, for you, honey."

"Like what?"

"You know, a loan or something."

"My grades ain't good enough for that."

"I ain't talking about grades. I'm talking about me and your father helping you out somehow."

"Dad can't do it and you know it."

82

There was a pause. Seems when I think back on it, words meant more then.

"Well, maybe I will."

She moved to hug me.

"Mom, you're gonna knock over the blocks."

"Oh, Jesus, I'm sorry. Is that what you want? 'Cause if you want to go to school, your daddy and I—"

"I don't know, alright?"

"You were just sayin'—"

"I said I don't know. Are you gonna stay here all night?"

She looked hard at me. Maybe she thought I meant was she gonna run out on Dad. Words again.

"No, no, I gotta do some things in the kitchen. How's your ankle?"

"It's okay. Can you get me something to drink?"

"Yeah, sure. Earl, honey?"

"Yeah?"

"You wanna keep the door closed if you're gonna have the TV on. Your Dad's a little cranky tonight."

I heard her walk quietly down the stairs, one of the saddest sounds that house could make. My old man was snoring, and it just got louder as Mom shut off the TV. I heard the chain pull on the light, but no more steps. She must've stood there in the dark a long time, listening to my old man snore, thinking, I don't know what.

Man, did I get out of that house the next afternoon. It looked like rain, one of those Ohio summer storms that old people always say makes the air feel "close" as they build up over the afternoon. Didn't matter to me. We had Muley's brother's car, a great metallic purple boat of a '75 Pontiac Bonneville with bench seats front and back. The beast had maybe one of the last steering wheel spinners in Ohio. I guess in the 50's and 60's everyone had one of these, but now they were rare. A little smaller than a hockey puck, the thing bolted on to the wheel, and you could hold it in your palm and steer with one hand. The other hand was free for your girlfriend's shoulder.

It was August, we had some money, and the radio worked.

Muley beeped the horn at Tim's father, who was cutting the grass. Mr. Matlock shut off his lawn mower and walked over to the car. He was the cool dad for us all, maybe not Tim, but the rest of us thought he probably let Tim drink beer sometimes at home and we knew he didn't hide his Playboys.

"Tim! Your friends are here! You boys up to no good again, I assume? How's that ankle, Earl? I heard all about you gettin' hurt. You lookin' forward to getting back to practice?"

"Doctor says I'm done for the season."

"Aw hell, Earl, that's too bad. What're you gonna do?"

"I don't know. Maybe watch practice, maybe help out Coach or something."

Tim hit the back seat, Mr. Matlock returned to his lawn, and Muley spun up backing out too fast. We drove twice past Rich's house honking the horn. But he was grounded for trying to steal from his dad's liquor cabinet.

"My dad told me all about your ankle. Shit, is Coach gonna be in a mood on Monday," said Tim over sound of the radio.

"I figured I'd walk over to practice and watch or something."

"Uh huh, cool, Earl. Hey are we still gonna get that case of beer? I got five bucks from my old man. You guys in?"

"Who's gonna get it?"

"Why don't we go to the Convenient Mart? If Mike's sister is working, we can get it for sure, like 99 times out of a hundred."

Parked the car, engine ticking in the heat. The three of us looked back at that metal beast, squinting to imagine three girls sitting on the big hood with enough room still left next to them to park a whole other car. But first was the beer. Mike's sister would never check for an ID if her boss wasn't around, so Tim went in with our money in ones and change. Mike's sister would cover you too, if you were a little short. We drove around some, drinking that warm beer. I remember my ankle hurt, how the thunderheads were building up to the west, how we had to hold the beer bottles down below the windows whenever we passed someone, how the radio sounded, how the asphalt smelled like summertime. Back then you waited for moments like this, but for that one second in time, I'd be happy to wait just as long again. Say what you want about small towns with nothing to do. But even though we never talked about anything more than girls and beer and what was on the radio, I thought at that moment I would hand over anything else I owned for another chance at doing that with those guys.

"Hey, shut up you guys." Muley brought us back to attention. It had just started to rain, weren't no regular soft summer rain, something that felt meaner, fat drops, making dust into mud on the windshield as we all turned at once like in a movie to see two girls run under the Dairy Queen awning to escape the downpour. Beer was good like syrup to us, but the promise of a teenage girl was magic.

"You know those two?"

"The one used to babysit with my sister sometimes," said Tim. "Muley, drive up there and offer them a ride."

"Yeah, c'mon, Muley."

"I ain't gonna do it. I don't even know them."

"C'mon, don't be a baby."

"I don't even know them. You ask them, Tim."

"Alright. Lemme in front." I went over the front bench seat into the back so Tim could move up.

Muley slowly glided that old Pontiac up to them girls. They saw us coming, probably from yesterday, but played it cool like girls were always better at than boys.

"Hey Cindy," said Tim.

"How you doing?"

"I'm fine. You need a ride somewhere?" Tim got held back in fourth grade and was older. He knew this kinda stuff.

"Who're you with in there?"

"This is my friend, um, Tom, and that's Earl. Where're you going?"

Since Tim was older, he knew not to call Muley by his nickname in front of girls and so called him Tom like his mom did.

"Where are you going?" Tim kept after them. "C'mon, it's rainin' and we got beer." They climbed in. Having a case of Stroh's, a decent car and some friends was like being James Bond in Reeve.

"What happened to your leg?" It was the cute one, pointing to my ankle. I guess I'd been rubbing it without thinking.

"Um, I hurt it during football practice."

Tim cut in. "Earl used to be on the Reeve team with me until he got hurt. Where do you two go to school?"

"Madison. We're just over here looking for something to do. Cindy's mom thinks we're babysitting." Not a bad start . . .

I caught Cindy checking her hair in the side view mirror. Okay...

She looked quickly toward her girlfriend. Maybe?

"You all got any more beer?" said Cindy.

Bingo.

"Ladies, keep your hands and feet inside the ride at all times 'cause it may get a little bumpy!"

This time the three of us boys went into the store together to get more beer. The two girls waiting in the car, using the rearview to smudge their makeup or something. Blue eye shadow was the thing that year. Tim and Rich ran in to the store first 'cause of the rain, while I got pretty wet moving as slow as I did with my ankle messed up. I was walking toward the back where they kept the beer when I overheard them.

"Shit, Tim. We got two girls waiting out there. Think we'll get home base tonight?"

"I don't know—sure as hell not with three of us around. We gotta ditch Earl."

"I feel bad, leavin' him in the rain and—"

"Yeah, I feel bad too, but you wanna get some tonight or what? C'mon, don't be a sissy."

They ran towards the front of the store with the twelve-packs of beer under their arms like footballs, threw money at Mike's sister behind the register and were back to the car with the urgency that only seventeen-year-old boys surfing waves of seventeen-year-old boy hormones and a lot of beer drunk too quickly could produce.

Dripping wet and with a long walk home in the rain, I counted my steps to the front door, barely said "Hi" to Mike's sister on the way out and, a little light-headed still from the beer I'd drunk earlier, started out across the parking lot, not giving much of a fuck about much.

IT WAS MOM here on the bus. She said to me:

That day was one of those days when it seemed as soon as I got the lunch dishes put away it was time for dinner.

"You worried about Earl?" I asked your dad. "About him losing his scholarship?"

"He never had no scholarship."

"You know what I mean, Ray."

"He don't need college. None of us did. Ain't nothing wrong with working with your hands for a living, maybe joining the service and learning a skill, growing up some like I did in Korea and my old man did in Germany. Traditions don't get to be traditions by accident, you know Sissy. Hell, it'd do the boy good, make a man outta him finally."

I ignored him and attended to cleaning up. I could hear the thunder outside and the lights flickered.

"Sounds like we're in for a doozy tonight. Hope the power stays on."

"I'm just concerned, Ray."

"And you're sayin' I'm not?"

"I ain't sayin' nothing about you."

"I care just as much about him as you do. But at least I'm not being impractical. Now goddamnit, I'm trying to watch TV, Sissy."

There was a long stretch of silence until the next commercial came on. We had to account for these things in our lives during sixty second breaks.

"I read in 'Dear Abby' tonight a letter from a wife whose husband has the same problem as us."

"We ain't got no problem."

"We do Ray. Lori said you even told Stan about it outside the Bowl America and that's why you two was mad at each other."

"To Hell with Stan, and to Hell with him again for telling Lori. I told you, we ain't got no problem."

"Dear Abby said in the paper to that lady that her husband should discuss it with their family physician or clergyman."

"Is that why you made the meatloaf tonight? To soften me up for this?"

"Ray—"

"Well, it didn't work. It didn't soften me up for nothing."

"I thought meatloaf was your favorite."

"It tasted like shit."

"I, well, I didn't have much time to get it ready. I'm sorry Ray. You know now I have to work all day waitressin' at that restaurant."

"Well maybe that ain't right neither. I told you before, Sissy. Now Monday you call that restaurant and quit. You tell 'em you're needed at home, which is true. A man can't raise his family when his wife's out all day."

"Ray, you know how things are."

"I've had enough with your working. You are gonna quit that job."

"No I ain't."

"How can you expect me to act like a man when you refuse to treat me like one. It ain't my fault—Stan was right—if you was more of a goddamn wife, I could be more of a husband."

"You're blaming this on me? The fact that you and me ain't slept like husband and wife for all this time is my fault?"

"Goddamn right. I'm going to get a beer."

"Don't you go into that kitchen."

"What?" Your dad said it like it was the first time he ever said the word out loud.

"I said, don't you go into that kitchen. You are gonna sit here and listen to me."

"Why—"

I was nearly hysterical, shouting over the rain and thunder at your dad.

"You are gonna sit here and goddamn listen to me. I ain't gonna take no blame, not no more Ray. I ain't gonna let you scream at me like I was some little girl you screwed after color guard practice. You remember that Ray? I was kneeling on the high school track waitin' to start marching and you walked up behind me and scared me, holdin' your hands over my eyes. I stood up and brushed the gravel off my knees, and Mrs. Reardon yelled at you, and you just acted so cool and calm and walked off. I had to take the blame for all that happened later, until your momma and daddy forced you to, but I ain't gonna take no blame for this. I am a proper wife, goddammit. I done everything I could for you, even wore that awful mail order

90

fancy underwear you made me wear. Said it would help, but it didn't, and I felt like a whore not no wife. And now you want me to quit work so you can feel like somebody you ain't no more. I ain't so stupid that I don't know. I am livin' and breathin' and—"

That was it. I broke down. I was done. The thunderstorm which began earlier in the evening had reached its peak so that my sobbing could hardly be heard by anyone that might have been listening. I fell back into the divan. Your dad Ray was standing, silhouetted in the kitchen doorway. A change had occurred in his face, something was broken there too when I looked up at him.

"What—" I said, more a gasp than a word by then. Ray had moved back into the shadow more, so I couldn't see him when he told me:

"Everything's dying around here; how can I be any different Sissy?"

He wandered off into the kitchen. I sat down in front of the television, commercials over, commercials back on.

JUST ME NOW, remembering that same night.

There was enough rain coming down to know God was angry too and talking back. I looked up, my face taking hard water, the storm reluctant to let me go. After a point, dragging my ankle through the rain, it was impossible to have been wetter. I wasn't cold, though. It was still summer, there was plenty of heat still held in the ground to burn off. I was near the bowling alley where my dad and all of them drank after work. I figured I could dry off, maybe find a ride home. I'd been in once or twice before, sent looking for Dad by Mom, but never went in for myself. You know, in a decent world that would have been the end of this night. I would have walked home, had dinner. Going to bed and waking up the next morning used to solve problems in the small town of Reeve, Ohio. But I was not really there anymore.

Instead, when I walked into the bar in that bowling alley, it turned out I was the most entertainment those old drunks had had all evening.

"Been swimming or something?"

"Ain't you a bit young to be drinkin' here?"

"I wish I was that young, so I could do more drinkin'."

"Why hell, it's Ray's boy! Hey there, Earl. I just knew with that ankle you'd be out on the town, not being in training no more."

"Yeah and gettin' laid. Christ, the pussy you young fellas get."

"So how you doin', Earl? You look all wet."

"If you're lookin' for your daddy, he ain't been in tonight."

"I came in to get outta the rain," I said, "and maybe for a drink."

"He really ain't in training."

"Don't bring him a glass of water. He's got enough of that already."

I thought maybe they'd put me out or something, but I was just accepted, no need for an initiation. Just showing up was enough; everyone could join the team. I realize now that in a way they were waiting for me, knowing sooner or later that we all ended up walking in one night. With that in mind, it was less of a surprise than I would've thought just a few hours ago when Mr. Matlock came out of the one toilet (there was no need for a ladies' room) and slapped money on the counter, paying for my beer.

"So how come you're so polite all of a sudden Matlock?"

"Same reason you're not, it's the way I was brought up. I just want to buy young Earl here a beer."

"That's generous of you," said one of them men. "You ain't never bought me a beer."

"Ah hell, quit your joking. Earl's a good boy," said Mr. Matlock, slapping me on my wet back. "I know he'll do the same thing for me someday."

MOM ON THE bus, remembering:

I was sitting alone in the darkened living room, TV on, but I was listening to the rain. I never heard Ray leave the kitchen, but he didn't answer me, so I tied my housecoat and walked over. The kitchen was dark save for the lightning that was slipping in through the windows and the orange dot of the timer on the stove. I tried at first to adjust my eyes, but instead turned on the overhead. It was a harsh light, and I was always after your dad to replace it with something nicer, but he never did. That night, it showed me Ray at the kitchen table, a half-empty liquor bottle beside him. A water glass full of whiskey nearby. He hardly ever drank much but beer, and I think we had that whiskey left over from a factory giveaway a couple of Christmases ago. The leftover Dairy Queen from before was spilled and dripping to the floor. I guess Ray had been eating it out of the container.

The only sound besides that storm was the splat-splat of the melting ice cream hittin' the floor.

"Ray, don't you—" I said to him, but he wasn't listening. I walked across the room to the sink, got a wet dish rag and wiped up the ice cream. What else was I to do? I sat down and poured myself a drink from Ray's bottle.

THAT'S WHAT MOM was saying to me on the bus, but in my head I was still at the bar, drinking with Mr. Matlock and two or three other men. Several empty beer pitchers sat on the table in front of us.

"So anyway," began one of the men, "The Big Bad Wolf jumps out and says, 'I'm gonna eat you, Little Red Riding Hood,' and she says, 'Eat, eat, eat. Doesn't anybody ever fuck anymore?'"

"Listen to this one. I was in bed with a blind girl last night and she said that I had the biggest dick she had ever laid her hands on. I said, 'Honey, you're pulling my leg.'"

"You hear the Irish Virgin's Prayer? Lord have Murphy on me."

"Boy sittin' with his girlfriend watching a stallion and a mare havin' at it. He says, 'I wish I was doing that right now.' Girl says, 'Go ahead, she's your horse.'"

"So how's it working out with that younger woman you're datin'?"

"She's added years to my life."

"Yeah, you look ten years older."

"This one guy says 'Why so down?" and the other answers 'Problems with the wife. She cut me back to only once a week for sex.' The first says 'Don't feel so bad, she cut all the other guys back too.'"

"So Earl," said one of 'em, "what, you figure you'll be droppin' out of school and looking for a job now that football's finished for you? I mean, why else stay in school, right? Hard times at the factory, but they might have something."

"Hell, leave him alone. The boy's only what, seventeen? Eighteen? He's gonna have his whole life to work, ain't you, Earl?"

"Earl, you tell your daddy to haul you down here tomorrow night again. The bunch of us can do some real drinking."

"Sounds good," said Mr. Matlock. "Well c'mon, Earl. I know you need a ride home."

Me and Mr. Matlock left the bar, got in his car.

"Your folks gonna be upset with you comin' home this late? Need me to say something to them for you?"

"Nah, it'll be okay."

Matlock hit a pothole big as a wading pool, mud up on to the windshield.

"I better watch out for them."

"For sure."

There was a long pause and the car traveled further on down the road.

"Was a time when Reeve was a better town."

"How's that, Mr. Matlock?"

"Life was like walking on ice. It took a little effort to keep from falling on your ass, but you could at least do it. Things are more uncertain now. Everything we used to figure was right, ain't. It's like change changed."

"You're gonna pass it."

"What's that, Earl?"

"My house, you're gonna pass it." Mr. Matlock was still pretty drunk, and started on about better times, thinking stuff old people do.

"I tell you, summers die Earl, summers die. When my own dad came home from the war, Japan was a wasteland along with Europe. Somehow we did to ourselves what the Krauts and the Japs couldn't. In Reeve, we had what we thought was a promise. The factory would give us jobs and we'd work hard for her. Nobody would be sleeping under the old Highway 61 railroad bridge like some do now."

"My old man told me he took two months to come home from the Japan war by boat and train and bus, walked into the house, kissed my mom on Friday, got blind ass drunk on Saturday, and went to work Monday, swearing that the best and worst days of his life always seemed to begin with a hangover. Jesus, money was everywhere. The factory was still making glass and houses were going up fast. When the work started to taper off, the Reeve family slipped some in how they ran the place—everybody remembers those years when lame old Harry Reeve was in charge, before his brother stepped in. But at least when the Reeve family made tough business decisions, they knew the families they'd be affecting."

"I put in a lot of good years alongside Stan and your dad. As hard as we worked, our product wasn't selling as much. The changes to the factory, more computer things and all, seemed necessary, but how can they expect a man to become high-tech when they don't pay for any education? Not much has changed in Reeve High School since I went there, and some of them textbooks you're using probably got my name still in them. Hell, Mrs. Reardon has been sixty-two for the last twenty years."

"We kept our part of the bargain, and we got played. The people who used our commitment realized they could take more and give us less. Wages went down 'to save our jobs.' Benefits went away 'to protect the company's future.' We all pushed our mortgages out, bought American cars, and now Reeve's gone. Nobody knows who owns that factory anymore. Maybe nobody owns it and it's just a ghost. There never was no bargain, they just kept telling us there was. We did our part, they slipped out the back door while we were wondering how we got from there to here. I don't know anymore, Earl. I wish I could think of some way to set it back right but it ain't gonna happen. Some people see this as a dismantling of the past, but I wonder if it isn't really just the future."

THE LIGHTS, WELL, some lights, were still on when I walked in the house. I wasn't sure if I was in trouble or not, so I was cautious entering the living room. I heard giggling. Walking through the house, I went to the kitchen, seeing Dad at the table with Mom on his lap, her arms wrapped around Dad's neck. I'd never seen them like that before, ever. They were both damn drunk and kissin' at each other, Mom stroking the hair at his temples, smiling delicately, like she was remembering something only she knew. An empty whiskey bottle was on the floor.

"We got company, Sissy."

"Who's that?"

"Looks like my fucking loser of a son, drunk like his old man."

"Earl, where you been?"

"I been out."

"Where's that?"

"At the bowling alley."

"Our boy's grown, you know that Ray," said Mom. "I remember when you was just a baby, little—"

"Sissy—"

"You was about three months old, and your daddy had you over his shoulder. Daddy was different then, still trying, don't be angry now Ray, it was like that then. And I heard him say, 'Look, I got a son.' Or how's about on the first day of school, when you walked home alone, and your Daddy hid in the bushes to be sure you'd be alright, embarrassed that you'd see him watching out for you. He loved you so much, Earl, was so happy putting you in the bath way back then. He'd take you as a baby to the park, push you on the swings saying, 'Back and a-wwwway, back and a-wwwway,' as you swung. Things changed, though, they did change."

"That's enough, Sissy. Earl, you better get off to bed, you came home too late. And tomorrow I'll take you down to the factory, see the foreman about a job. Shit, fall's almost here already," he said, and I just went up the stairs, leaving them alone with their drink and the last of the summer and each other.

Industrial Waste

I LOOKED FOR work in all the places. The worst part was the first contact. You walked in and the store people smiled at you, thinking you were gonna buy something, "May I help you sir?" and then as soon as you mentioned a job, the smile dropped hard and you were no longer wanted and if they even continued to say "sir" it sounded sarcastic. A few would send you off with an application form they'd toss unread later, or, as time went on, push you away to a web site. Most Korean-run businesses that had opened in Reeve had no use for anyone outside their families, and the State liquor store hired from outside town, about the lowest rung on the ladder of political favors you could buy by helping elect the governor. I took to hanging around the parking lot, what we joked was called the slave market, talking with others there, all of us convinced we'd gather in case someone would come looking for day help. They'd come in from Mars, I figured, because there was no reason I could think of why anyone in town would need our labor. Still, sometimes someone would need something done and I made a few bucks. I cut grass and delivered newspapers, jobs I did now as an adult that I used to do for pocket money as a kid. I was a member of the "working poor," words that are a profanity together.

Another one way to get by for me was pay day loans. A shop set up business in the strip mall. If you could show you had pay stubs from some sort of job, and they were easy enough to borrow or fake, and the shop guy never looked too close anyway, you could get a short-term loan to cover you until the next pay check. Anybody could get one, not like a credit card or a proper bank loan. The problem was you paid a $15 charge on every $100 borrowed, but if you didn't pay it back on time it got big fast, zooming up to 390 percent a year. Something like two out of every ten people never paid it back at all, and the shop owner said he charged the rest of us more because of that. I asked him about the damn interest rate, and he said that borrowing from him cost less than the fee on a bounced check, knowing that kiting checks at the end of the month was another poor man's way of "borrowing money." Still, it was important to get the cash, especially after Ohio started locking up people who couldn't pay off their parking tickets. Ain't no judge or court in them cases either, it's all administrative.

Soon enough it wasn't just these store-front bastards doing it, the big name banks got in on it too. They called it a better name, like "Early Access" or "Ready Advance," and said it was a kind of civic service, a short-term solution for money emergencies. But the average borrower took out thirteen of these emergency loans a year until it all caught up with him. The loan was supposed to be paid automatically by direct deposit. However, if your money was short, the bank stuck you with fees and even more interest on the unpaid part until you cycled down into a hole so deep you'd never pay it out. There was almost no way to get ahead of it once you started down that road, and the banks knew it.

Celebrated one Labor Day by borrowing against my car title. You could get half the value of your car in cash the same day. If you couldn't pay it back on time, they'd give you an extension, at a higher rate. Rates was high to begin with; at that time it was close to one hundred percent interest, but now a lot of states protect working men by limiting the rate to only thirty percent. Still, for most, it all led to a cycle of debt with the constant repo threat overhead. When you failed to pay up and they called the loan, you lost the car. Try and keep the car anyway, they report it as stolen and the cops'll go pick it up for them, throwing you in jail for stealing your own car at no extra charge. Who the cops working for, right?

I couldn't qualify for a credit card, the middle class way of borrowing money. Those people pay like twelve to fifteen percent interest, so not a helluva lot different from payday loans. Just looks cleaner. I also bypassed those fuckin' rent-to-own thieves, who let you rent a TV or a washer and dryer until you paid them a lot more than the appliance is worth and it's old, at which point you own the thing, dropping $450 on a $200 item 'cause you had no choice but to pay over time and nobody else would give you credit. There's whole industries out there that sprang up because us working poor became a new market.

With that in mind I even tried to cash in on it myself, working briefly for a collection agency. When folks could not pay, the debt got sold down the line. Some big bank wasn't gonna fuss over small change, so it sold the debt to a big agency, who sold it to a smaller one like I worked for, a place that might see profit in getting twenty percent of a two hundred dollar collection. At those rent-to-own joints, you ended up having to sign tons of papers, all looking like they was written by a Keep Lawyers Employed committee, so that if you miss a payment the store takes back the whole appliance, not just the half they still own. This scared the dumb asses renting, but actually the last thing that company wanted was to repo a two-year-old TV, so my job was to knock on the door and try to get them to pay something, and at the same time see if they'd refinance at an even higher rate. Loan to pay a loan, how's that sound? That old TV was worth nothing to us, but was some kind of magic shittin' thing to some old lady. If she was a single mom, the TV was her babysitter—feed your sister after Wheel of Fortune, lights out after Idol—and she wasn't gonna give it up easy. When I talked them into an even more fucked-up refi deal that let them keep the TV, they'd usually thank me for helping them out. Sometimes them moms would offer me what we called a couch payment, head or bed in return for me to report to the boss no one home. My last customer was a returned soldier who owed $100 for a bicycle he was buying over time for his daughter's ninth birthday. Fuck if I was gonna repo a Barbie two-wheeler with pink streamers on the handle bars. I quit the job that day. No one home in this part of America.

After my old man died I got his, well, actually his own dad's, gold watch. I was never gonna wear it hanging around parking lots, and could care less about remembering him more anyways, so I ended up at one of Reeve's new pawn shops. These things have been around elsewhere since God invented dirt, but really took off as the economy tanked. It works pretty simply. You walk in with something, and they give you a "loan" of usually ten to twenty-five percent of actual worth and a ticket receipt. If you can pay back the loan, plus interest, in ninety days, you get your thing back. If not, the shop takes your item and sets in a display case and tries to sell it. Seems pretty straight, basically gettin' loaned money at 75-90 percent interest.

Only what really happens is this. I walk in with that watch, at least halfway hopeful thinking I'm gonna snag some quick cash. Instead, soon as I cross the door frame I am nine years old again, sneaking with Muley, Tim and Rich into my mom and dad's bedroom, pulling open his moth-ball-smelling (Mom protected the house against a plague's worth) underwear drawer and showing them that gold watch. We had just seen a pirate movie and were all full of talk about gold and treasure, and that was about the most valuable thing I thought we owned. The group of us looked at it, turning it over in the light, feeling how heavy it was. It was a magical thing, more a jewel than a watch, something from another time. It glowed new because it was old. We had seen all sorts of "gold" things, but I think that was the first time we had held anything that was real gold, heavy, cold, valuable. We were gonna actually put it in a model car box and bury it in the yard to dig up later playing pirates until we heard my mom coming up the stairs with laundry and I shoved it back into the drawer and ran to my room with my friends. I think I almost wet myself that day, it was all so exciting.

Standing in the dark pawn shop, the guy inside the sales cage gave me the hairy eyeball, I guess thinking maybe I stole the watch or something. Like he cared. He looked at it, checked some catalog, weighed it on an ancient old scale with little weights like chess pieces, and said twenty bucks. Twenty bucks. My grandpa, my dad, me nine years old, or food money for four or five days if I skimped. Two nights of beer if I didn't. I asked him for more and he said twenty bucks, this ain't a yard sale. I remembered my dad near the end, holding that watch. "I can't remember anything anymore," he told me. "You can," I said. "That's the point of a thing like this." It stood in for everything that was missing. I started to tell the pawn shop guy about my dad, and he turned his back on me. He'd heard it all and had no interest. Just business. "You want stories?" he said. "I got people coming in here pulling their wedding rings off their fingers tryin' to pawn them. You wanna tell someone your story? Find a preacher who cares."

Twenty bucks. That same day I also bought some lottery tickets and stood outside in a thunderstorm, as I had an equal chance of winning and being hit by lightning and couldn't decide which I'd prefer. The pawn shop stole from me, but to get by it was either let him or I'd of had to steal from someone else. I learned you could rob someone with a pen as easily as a gun.

Since the businesses we worked for could get away with not paying us enough to live on, other businesses popped up to loan us money at rates we could never afford to pay back because of course the businesses we worked for could get away with not paying us enough to live on. Then the government started subsidizing the businesses to not pay us enough to live on with food stamps, aid to babies, that sorta thing—with our own tax money that they took from our wages at those same businesses. Cream in coffee, just swirls around and down. Companies stopped sharing the profits of labor with the workers who increased the productivity and instead just shoveled the money upstairs so we can't afford to buy what we make. Now if we're not workers and we're not consumers, what are we?

SO HERE'S MY life. You gotta watch the alcohol and the drugs if you're living rough. First of course is that they are expensive—there's no Dollar Menu at the liquor store—and once you start down that road it slides under you too fast. You drink a little to stay warm, you drink a little to pass the hours. You accept a passed joint to be friendly, and pretty soon life starts to feel better disconnected. Mornings were there to sleep through, afternoons that had no purpose. You start to wonder who made the rule about no drinking until 5 p.m., or 3 p.m., until there is no reason not to drink whenever now is. Shame ain't no problem, as it'll go away at least until morning after the third drink. Then she starts to take your money, then you start eating even less and pretty soon you're that guy on the bench with a paper bag wrapped around a jolt of malt liquor from the gas station. I tried to stay clear of the drugs; beer was always our drug then in Reeve anyway, and from time to time I do admit I took comfort in the songs at the bottom of those bottles.

You acquire a different sense of time. You get tired jobless in a way that sleep don't fix. You wait a lot, waiting not for a movie to start but just waiting, waiting for something to change or just for another day to end. Near the bottom, before you disappear under the alcohol, there's the problem of what to do with all that time. When I had a life it was always about not having enough time. Homeless, too dirty for places that sell things, you got time. Libraries are good but you can't overdo it and in a small town with only one, closed half the fucking time anyway 'cause of budget cuts, it's not a full-time job. Sitting or sleeping only covers so much territory, so you end up walking around. At first you just start doing it, unsure how long you can stay on your feet, 'til you end up staggering like a drunk. That's funny, yeah? Sometimes I used to ride the public buses around town—now, that's also funny—as they were dry and warm. Some drivers would let you on for free, some didn't even want to touch the crumpled up dollar from your pants pocket, some would make you pay a little and let you stay on until the end of their shift. Some assholes would see you stand in the fucking snow just 'cause you couldn't pay the full fare. They're afraid of losing their own jobs for helping someone. Just like that fucker truck driver who wouldn't gimme a ride when I walked away from Angie.

I was flat-out drunk one night when she crept back into my head. I don't know what the hell made this night any different than the others. It was probably my new girlfriend Ms. Budweiser because I was drunker than shit, but I dug some coins outta my jeans and went to a pay phone. In those days when dinosaurs roamed the land around Reeve, we had pay phones, they cost a dime and you could talk to a person at "information" to find a number.

"As our valued customer, your call is important to us, please hold."

"Hello? Hello, I wanna, um, want to, yeah, talk to Angie."

"Name and city, sir?"

"Her fuckin' name is Angie like I just said. She lives maybe near that Greenwich Village. Gimme that number."

"Which city in Ohio, sir?"

"It's New York, New York the city, I just wanna talk to her dammit."

"Yes sir, New York City. Transferring to long distance information now—"

"As our valued customer, your call is important to us, please hold."

"New York information, may I help you, last name please?"

"Angie goddammit. Angela, Angel. Soft shoulders, you know, the one from the parking lot . . . "

"Last name or address please, sir?"

"She sent me a fucking postcard sayin' she fucking lives looking out the window at a park, so gimme that address. Goddammit, help me."

The operator hung up. I slept it off. Things always look better in the morning.

REEVE LOST OUT on the big Bullseye retail store, when Gibbsville offered better tax breaks to the company plus a couple years' free lease on the old high school land after they closed the second high school due to fewer students and people moving away. The company built there what is called a big box store.

The idea was our tax money was used to lure that company in, and they was smart enough to play Reeve off against Gibbsville like we did in football, when all along they knew they were gonna locate somewhere around here anyway. It was our tax money being used to create jobs for us. They held a job fair, with tables set up in the other high school's gym, decorated with magic marker-written signs and a few tired balloons, which was all that stood for the fair part. A lot of people were already lined up when I got there, and the Bullseye people were wearing their bright blue vests walking around, looking us over like livestock. We covered a lot of ground, from last year's model of homecoming queen to retired guys who couldn't afford to retire. "Interested in loading dock?" they said to me, "C'mon over and talk about cosmetics here," they'd say to the pretty high school girls. We were good little pieces of meat.

One guy said that because Bullseye drove his small store outta business he had to take a minimum wage job at Bullseye, which only pays him enough so that he sorta has to buy at Bullseye. They made him a greeter at the front door and told him to be enthusiastic. He was. Like that, all them jobs wasn't much. You got one and you were happy at first, but you soon felt like you made it onto one of the life boats from the Titanic but were just waiting for the next big wave to dump.

My job at Bullseye was to take big boxes of things off the truck, and do the break down. It was called officially by Bullseye in the associate handbook, "Inbound Event Processing." What happened is that a computer at the Bullseye headquarters called a computer at a warehouse, which notified a computer in New Jersey to send off a buy order ultimately to a factory computer in Thailand to make some more headache pills to replace the ones we had ordered for our store. They came in a big carton of say 144 smaller boxes. I tore a pick sheet off the printer, which told me to count out thirty-six of them boxes into a plastic tub labeled PHARMACY, then count out say twenty-four more and put them into a tub labeled GROCERY, and so forth. Somebody else would come into the back room from each of those departments and take their tub. Because of me and my counting, the Bullseye store could order a big cheap box of 144 and I'd divide them up right. A computer could not do that and so almost reluctantly I had a job.

The day I lifted that first box off the truck, I felt something. My eyes saw the pick sheet, and I found the carton. My arms lifted it up and while it wasn't heavy, it had some weight, enough that I could feel the muscles work. My strength was challenged a bit, not just lifting food into my mouth, but lifting weight because a man was paying me to do that. Hadn't seen you in a while, old friend, hello.

The job was real easy to learn. There was no apprentice system needed here, no paid jobs for boiler operators' assistants, no plumber's helpers. I walked in and Steve, the Team Leader, said "Take the pick sheet there, go to the truck, hit them with that barcode scanner gun, count them out right, initial the pick sheet and put it in that folder. Fifteen minute break's at noon. No talking, but you can wear head phones as long as you're in the back room. Come in to work through the rear entrance, never use the front door or park in a guest space. Late from break twice and you're fired. Bullseye welcomes you as a valuable addition to our team, um, Earl." He'd looked up just at the end of my welcoming speech and seen my name tag. Steve the Team Leader was hard to get to know. He stayed in his office most of the time, and when we had these mandatory team-building meetings, he'd say stuff to us that sounded like he was reading lines from a play written by Bullseye, like "So how's the [insert popular local sports team name] doing, [insert teammate's name]?" It was almost like Bullseye didn't want him to think much. Maybe us neither.

On my first day, I met with Teri, from Human Resources. She told me I had to decide how Bullseye would pay me. See, Bullseye wanted everyone to use electronic direct deposit, which was the cheapest, well, Teri said best, thing for Bullseye and thus for its valued team members. Problem is that to use direct deposit you had to have a place to deposit into directly, a bank account. That used to be simple, and as a kid I remember being walked into the bank one Saturday morning with a bag of quarters and some paper birthday money to open my first passbook savings account. The old guy banker even let me keep the pen I used to sign things. Now, banks want chunky minimum amounts to open an account, and want to charge you for checks and stuff. If you don't maintain some heavy balance, they charge fees, so for a guy like me banks were too expensive. You also needed a mailing address and ID to prove you were just homeless and not a homeless terrorist. "No problem," said Teri from Human Resources, "Bullseye understands and for a $7.95 biweekly courtesy fee will gladly issue you a paper check."

I would then have to take the check to a storefront check cashing place (again, no bank account), which charges a courtesy fee of four percent largely because they could care less if you're a homeless terrorist as long as they get their share. "No problem," said Teri from Human Resources, "Bullseye understands and will pay you in the form of a debit card. It looks just like a regular credit card, and every two weeks your salary gets loaded on it electronically, automatically." I could even manage it on-line, if I had an on-line. Cool, so I did that. Only I found out that to get actual cash I had to stick the thing into an ATM for a fee, and if the balance fell below a minimum, fee, and there was a monthly maintenance charge fee, so basically if I didn't spend it quick enough in the right way my money evaporated. The only place I didn't pay a fee to spend my own money was if I used the card at Bullseye. Even just getting my hands on my money I'd earned was like trying to pick up a turd by the clean end.

Teri also guided me through my drug test. Most places that don't pay much seem really concerned that their workers are drug-free. I'm not sure why this is, 'cause I learned that you can be a banker or lawyer and get through the day higher than Jesus on a cloud. Regardless, for the first time since Muley and me peed off the Black River Bridge drunk together on my birthday, I urinated in front of another person, handing him the warm cup. He gave me one of those universal signs of the underemployed I now recognized, a "we're all in it, what're ya gonna do" look, just a little upward flick of his eyes. Even though I was hung over as hell, I did pass thanks to alcohol not being part of the test.

Then I had to buy some blue, collared shirts and what my mom would've called khaki slacks, which were the uniform for Bullseye. I got to keep and wash the uniform, which was okay I guess, but even with the employee discount it meant that I worked my first two days just to buy the clothes they wanted me to have. As a kid I used to get all my clothes at Christmas mostly, except for jeans and T's, but you had to be pretty rich to wear jeans and a T to work. Bullseye was pretty strict on the uniform, except for Courtney the Cosmetics Girl, who was allowed to wear a scoop neck, I guess because the assistant manager liked her, and she had big boobs and the customers liked that. She approached her job with all the enthusiasm of a kid's toy whose batteries were about to die, but she had big boobs and that was enough.

Teri from Human Resources last help to me was a video on theft. Bullseye was deeply concerned for the welfare and well-being of its valued associates and thus maintained a drug-free environment, but it seemed equally concerned for its own welfare and well-being, as the video warned me about stealing anything. The interesting thing is that, in addition to warning us about stealing candy and pop for breaks, we were not to steal time from Bullseye. Bullseye paid us for our time and so even if we snuck out for a smoke or flipped through a magazine chatting up a checkout girl, we were stealing their time. Would we have liked someone from Bullseye to come to our home (or, I guess, motel room, car back seat, shelter bunk or cardboard box under a bridge) and have to do whatever the hell Bullseye would want from us there? Bullseye's rules reminded me of church, where pretty much whatever we wanted to do turned around to be a sin. How the preacher could read young men's minds was unclear, but Bullseye seemed to have the same knack. The good news was, oriented, I was ready to go to work. But one more thing—it turned out that this orientation was unpaid, done before we were technically hired, and so it was considered an investment in ourselves and our future, Teri said.

It was hard to get to know the other workers, the associates, as we were told not to talk and because it turned out that Steve the Team Leader had another computer. His computer wasn't hooked up to the headache pill factory but instead was watching those pick sheets. As I came to learn, the bar code scanner was kind of watching over me. The people who came and picked up my filled tubs had one too, and those scanners told Steve how fast I was picking and filling. On days when I apparently wasn't doing those things fast enough, Steve would come out and tell me I was not performing to my full potential as a valued teammate and that meant I had to work faster. I did. I did not have his computer, so I wasn't sure how fast was right, or fast enough, and so I tried to just do it all as fast as I was able. But no mistakes—Steve was angry, sure, if I was slow, but if I put too many or too few into a bin and the bar code scanner told him, that made him especially angry. It was my job to pick and sort stuff, but it was Steve's job to make sure Bullseye made money, he said. That was what I came to know as management. Steve was actually about my own age, but he had come from Louisville with the Bullseye corporate family, and I always kinda thought of him as a lot older than me. I was pretty sure his last name was Manning or Marvin, but he was also always insisting that as a teammate I was to only call him Steve or I'd be in trouble for that too. Still, it was better than when I worked off-the-books for a while in the craft store at Christmas, coming home like a stripper with a pocket full of ones and fives covered in glitter.

I tried chatting up this older woman named Patty, but all she did was complain. Bullseye had a computer watching her work, too.

"I started at the end of October as just a cashier. So alright, they got this speed time shit that measures how long you take ringing guests up. They want you to be in green as much as possible because that means you are fast. Red means you are slow. The problem with their system is that it is not always your fault. At first I heard about how you can cheat by suspendin' the transaction if the guest is taking too long, but you're only supposed to do that when you're waiting on like a price check. You can't do it too much, or the computer'll tell on you for that. Sometimes a guest will slide their card, but they will take a freakin' eternity to answer the credit card questions, which ruins my speed score. I kid you not when I say some guests take literally a full minute to finish it and it's like one damn question—credit or debit. So apparently that is my fault now too."

The next Tuesday, as Patty was getting fired, she found out that the cash registers also counted out ring time for items per minute, tender time for the space between finishing the ringing up and putting money in the drawer, her idle non-sale time plus customers per hour, items per hour and sales per hour. Whatever numbers were good for all that she didn't have. So no one really saw her do nothing wrong, but she got fired by the computer. They posted each cashier's scores in order next to the break room so you sorta could guess who'd be fired next.

Patty also always told us she was actually an artist. Her terrible paintings of seascapes taken from pictures in some book decorated the walls at Lewis' Pizza, where customers could buy them, assuming they showed up for pizza with two hundred extra dollars shopping for an oil painting. No effort had been spared to make those pictures awful, and I grew up five hundred miles inland. I guess Patty was still good looking in that older bat shit crazy chick kinda way, but in truth, that relationship wasn't going nowhere. Damaged, restock pile.

Now the Cart Guy at Bullseye was pretty funny. His job was to rodeo the carts outside the store. That's it, but it still seemed to confuse him some days. Reminded me of Muley, who had joined the Army and left Reeve. Cart Guy must've put in five miles a day in the parking lot, summer and winter, rain and snow, and his feet was all calloused from the running. He used to stub out cigarettes against his bare heel in the break room to make us laugh. Great stories about long nights out, painting the floor with IHOP pancakes and vodka. He'd always do imitations of the guests, sayin', "Excuse me, EXCUSE ME Sir, freaking excuse me, SIR." He said one time, not fully joking, "Did you know 'No Shirt, No Service' applies to employees too?" Cart Guy's cigarette trick got old and so that wasn't going anywhere either, because the kid was like nineteen and even I could see he was already pretty much dead without knowing it. More damaged goods, return to vendor.

This girl named Leigh missed one day. She told Kevin the Store Manager she misread the schedule. Kevin said if she didn't have no doctor's note then one more time and she was gonna get excused, get back to work, have a good day. Excused was the word Bullseye used instead of fired, like us being valued associates instead of just workers. Words sort of meant something different inside Bullseye, like they never really wanted to make it clear what they meant. Kevin the Store Manager said one time he had worked twelve years for Bullseye, so he knew the special meaning words, and the rules and the tricks, and got to be the boss. Kevin the Store Manager loved rules. He was probably the only person who really didn't stick Q-Tips in his ears just because the box said not to. Rules made him feel comfortable by making his choices smaller. At the same time, he'd flirt clumsily with the high school worker girls, and they'd flirt back without enthusiasm thinking it might be good for their jobs in some still-developing pubescent version of being nice to the boss. Everybody learned fast. Kevin had as his big responsibilities making sure the pricing guns were racked at the end of each shift, and doing bag searches for the cashiers on the way out the door so they wouldn't steal. You could guess that this wasn't Kevin's dream job. It was nobody's dream job. It was just somewhere you ended up and, if you were tired or unlucky, got stuck.

Out in the parking lot, this young guy with a clipboard came up.

"Hey, you got a minute? I'm from the union, wanna talk with you about a meeting we're having soon."

"Get away. We heard about you at the last team-building exercise. They said to stay away or we'd get fired. Said you can't even be in this parking lot, it's private property of Bullseye."

"Just give me a minute. C'mon, they're paying you, what, $4.25 an hour? Hell, that's what a fast food lunch you gotta eat in your 15 minutes of break costs. Is that really what an hour of your labor, man, your life, is worth?"

"Mister, back off. We ain't got much but these jobs. We're scared. Some of us got kids and all of us got bills. We can't afford to go to your meeting. Now leave us be with this." Jeez, that union guy was out there all the time, even when it was raining. I couldn't for the life of me understand why someone would be standing there in the rain then. Must have been somethin' in it for him.

We all got little pins yesterday, as our store sold over one million dollars in stuff. Anyway, Bullseye got a million dollars, and I got a little pin to stick on my name tag, which I must wear. New thing: Everyone has to memorize the five rules of superior customer service and recite them on demand from Kevin the Store Manager. He actually walks around the store and stops us, saying, "Earl, tell me Rule Number Three." Rule Three is, "Ask the guest if she has found everything she desires." The hard part is about half the warehouse staff speak Spanish, and memorizing the rules is really hard for them. Thank you for listening to this and please come again (adapted by me from Rule Five).

New break policy: zero to five and a half hour shift, no break. New schedule policy: all shifts reduced to five and a half hours or less. Somebody said it was illegal not to give us breaks, but what can you do, call the cops like it was a real crime? Well, turns out the joke's on me. I asked that union guy out in the parking lot about it, and he explained to me that we were in a "Right to Work" state. By law, employers are not required to grant breaks to anyone over age 16; Bullseye gives us some kinda break, but in other places minimum wage workers like us do eight and nine hour shifts without a meal or a chance to get off their feet for a few minutes. No one gets sick leave, holidays, or vacation time, of course.

I actually asked Kevin the Store Manager about this. He was always encouraging us to talk to him about anything. "My door is always open," he said, before going into his office and closing the door. One time I knocked, and standing in the doorway I asked him about having a break more often, just a few minutes to sit down and take a load off, and Kevin the Store Manager said:

"You're lucky to have this job. Lotta people out there who'd take your place."

"I know Kevin, and I'm grateful. I'd just like a chance to sit down and eat a regular lunch on them long shifts."

"Well, we all gotta do what is best for Bullseye. Careful you don't bite the hand that feeds you."

I got it. Even if I'm never fed.

People not caring like that let the bullies get in charge. Seemed familiar. When I was a kid I really believed the border between me and the world leaked both ways, so that I could maybe affect things instead of just being affected by them, but it's different now when you work for a big company like Bullseye. At that point you realize that not everything is possible, and that changes everything.

❧   ❧   ❧

God only knows how it made its way from wherever it was grown to Reeve. I doubt they had a computer that ordered dope from a factory in Thailand like Bullseye, but it must've been something like that. Weed never took, though, not like beer and whiskey. It was expensive, it made you want to eat, which cost more money, it made you kind of sleepy later, and it wore off too fast after that. Not a Midwest kind of drug. The state of Ohio had the booze monopoly, retailing everything but beer and wine itself in the State stores. Taxed it to hell, too, what was called a sin tax. What they counted on was that tolerance to alcohol developed pretty fast. You drank to get drunk most times around here, but it kept taking more and more to get to the same place. That was a good business model for the sellers, but had its downside for the buyers.

So there was meth. Meth was cheap, really cheap, and you could make it in Ohio, a new industry. Anybody could do it, just use a recipe and add in stuff from decongestants from the drug store and solvents and salts. Making meth with this shit can result in explosions and toxic gas, a business risk. But, be careful, and follow the instructions people who paid attention in high school chemistry class wrote, and all of a sudden you're an entrepreneur. Meth wasn't a social drug, and so you didn't need to hang around with old juicers in a dark bar. Meth came to you. Your friends were using it, if not selling it or cooking it, and the angry, speedo high it gave fit the young guys better. Meth wasn't only for boys, either. Girls liked it too, and 'cause you never thought about eating on a meth cruise, they called it the Jenny Crank diet.

Butane lighter and a glass tube, or just smoke it off a hot light bulb, "will get you homeward bound ridin' the pipe," they'd say while they could still talk straight. We even had a bit of tradition from way, way back of making moonshine in the woods, so that fit too.

Meth and what happened to Ohio were just waiting for each other. I tried it a couple of times—everybody did—like a new restaurant in town most folks would eat there at least once, so they could talk about it with their friends. For a world stuck in shit, meth was the answer. This was a drug designed for unemployed people with crappy self-images and no confidence. And that was it. Meth wasn't about having drugs, it was about not having no jobs. It don't seep into your brain like weed, it comes in like an iron man fist. Imagine the feeling you get from the one thing that interests you the most, especially at that first hit of the session, zero-to-sixty. Imagine what it feels like to be the smartest, or the strongest, or the sexiest person in the world. Remember the most excited and energetic you've ever felt. Man, you feel like you accomplished stuff before you even got started, your brain running in crazy fast nervous wicked noisy circles. You wanna do everything at once, flying on the buzziness of the confusion. You are horny as hell, and it is so fucking good you bite a hole in your lip, and when you get off, it feels like only minutes speeded by. Get some clean stuff and handle it right, you could keep altitude for hours. Now, take all of these things and multiply them by a thousand or a million and there you have the feeling of meth. Until it fades. Then you blink away the dust and you're back on the couch without a job or a hope in hell and not having slept or ate, and feeling inside like everyone you ever cared about just died. Then you just gotta do it again, only it takes just that much more. You of course started with just a taste or two and then you find yourself buying more weight, from a guy you don't know with a gun in his belt, and you realize you're now inside the reality that used to stay behind the curtain. See the problem? See the profit?

Jodie continued talking.

"Chris said at first he just wanted to play around cooking the stuff in the basement, like a hobby sort of, tryin' it out to see if he could do it. But somewhere his hobby turned into a felony. He was bringing home money, but he was more and more violent towards me and the boys. He'd slap at me outta frustration and I understood, but with the boys most of the time it was real rage. I think because they were still young and Chris saw they still had a life ahead, that made him hate them. Meth made him angry right off, but then he'd see something on TV about jobs going, or some commercial for something he wanted, and he'd just turn purple. The boys would do something kids do, you know, trying to get Chris off the couch during the day to play or to get them some jelly sandwiches while I was working, and he'd just lash out at them with his fists. I knew he didn't realize how hard he'd hit them, but they were just kids, you know, and it scared me more than not having money. Lotta rotten in those times, but then he'd say, 'Come over here,' when he wanted to make up with me, but I'd already been there. It was a hard calculation, but one night when Chris was out I packed up what I could, took as much of his shit as I could find, put the boys in the car and left. We spent a couple of nights out, spent some time with my sister, and after I sold Chris' gun and stupid man-bracelet, we got a small place. At first I worried he'd show up some night, but he didn't. Deputy Sheriff came to the house twice, once looking for him on a skipped warrant, once to tell me they'd found him, wrapped around a .45 hollow point."

"The future scared me. I think it was only my own cowardice and the thought of what would happen to the kids that kept me alive. So this Bullseye job is a Godsend. I had no medical insurance and pay $60 a month on an $8,000 medical bill from after I fell. I just hurt my ankle, but going into the emergency room costs. I'll have it paid off in maybe seven or twelve years, if things go well. I gotta pay on it so that I can go back to the hospital with the boys when I need to. If I don't pay, they list me into collection and the hospital won't touch me. This way though, I'm working one day a week for the hospital really. Not sure how to get ahead 'cause Bullseye caps us at thirty nine hours a week so we're not full-time employees that receive benefits. Seems they just hire more part-timers instead of letting anyone jump to full time. I keep telling the Team Leader I just need more hours, not the benefits, but he only thanks me for my contribution, like I can feed my boys that shit. Then they keep changing which hours I work each week, so I never can plan nothing and it's hard to have a second job. I got an hour bus ride here and an hour back, so when I get just a three hour shift it's hardly even worth it. My friend at Jimba Juice, she says they even factor the weather reports into scheduling, so when the temperature drops shifts get cut without any notice."

Bullseye was okay enough for me about the schedule though, as pretty much everyone who could find one worked at least two jobs. Had to. If the other job would agree to always give you

Friday hours, then Bullseye would block those out. They as a business really adapted to this new economy thing, gotta give them credit. Only problem was on holidays, when everyone wanted workers in, and of course weekends, when people with better jobs were free to come out and consume. Bullseye had an electronic time clock. It wouldn't let you punch in more than five minutes early, and if you were more than five minutes late it'd send a message to your supervisor. You got deducted half a point for that; get six points in a six-month period and you were automatically fired. If you got three points in six months, the supervisor was required to give you a verbal warning, which they took way too seriously. If you called in sick, it was one point off, so most everyone came in coughing and sneezing no matter what. You also couldn't clock out late, even if you were in the middle of something you were told to finish or else. You had to put it down, clock out on time, and then go back to finish up off the clock, 'cause even five minutes of unauthorized overtime bought you a half point off. Coming and going. It wasn't about the money, 'cause at minimum wage the minutes were only worth pennies to Bullseye—it was about reminding us we should do what we were told to do.

That was it, right there. The trick to doing a good job was to learn how to do just a good enough job. Too much thinking and you'd surely step on some Bullseye rule, or cross some invisible line Kevin the Store Manager felt strongly about in his heart. You had to pay attention, but not too much. Enough time in this retail minimum economy and it was trained into you for life, but for newcomers like me it was a slow process of getting pushed back into the ground every time we had an accidental growth spurt. None of us were trying to be great, just satisfied.

Guests, which was a Bullseye word for what we used to call customers, were something. They were us, but a damn darker version of us. One of them made one of the high school girl associates cry, saying she was gonna ruin her kid's birthday because we sold the last of some stupid ass toy before she got there. Kevin the Store Manager came over and apologized, stepping right between the red-faced consumer and the crying valued associate, promising a rain check special order and a swift and courteous checkout when the time came. Another one threatened to call the police on us because we closed earlier than he said we said we would.

Funny thing happened one time. I was walking in to work, hat and jacket on outside so no one could see my Bullseye nametag and all. Some woman bumped into me by accident. She turned and apologized, said something about the weather getting colder and said sorry again, smiling. I then saw her like ten minutes later inside the store, me dressed as a Bullseye associate and her pushing a shopping cart. She almost ran over me, but didn't say a word. Me, a person in the parking lot, but just an item inside.

I had to work closing one time. Walking out to my car, which was still working at that time, with the others across the open empty parking lot, Kevin the Store Manager called me. I don't think he remembered my name, because he said, "Hey Ryan," but he said it towards me, so I walked over anyway. He saw me parked right there, and said employees couldn't park closer than thirteen rows to the store so that the good close spaces would be for guests. I wasn't sure what to do. I thought about asking him why thirteen rows and not twelve or fourteen, but I thought about it more and remembered it was better not to think about it. Then I noticed I was the only car parked anywhere near the front of the store. Everyone else but me believed already.

This one older guy worked with us. He didn't talk much, but said he used to be an accountant who got retired and then worked on the floor at Bullseye providing superior customer service because he had no pension. One day this customer like half his age called him stupid and said, "I suppose there's a reason people like you have to work in places like this." Somehow that set him off, and right in front of Kevin the Store Manager the old guy said, "fuck you" to the customer and, "I quit" to Kevin the Store Manager. The guy said to me on the way out that he doubted the woman he told to fuck off learned anything and that she likely took some pleasure in seeing him quit, no doubt a validation of her own superiority. I said "okay" because my break was ending and I couldn't be late back to my station, especially with Kevin the Store Manager likely in a shitty mood.

Then one day Jodie really got beaten up on by a customer. She wanted something we were out of, and Jodie told her we were out. The lady just lit up: "Where's the manager, why won't you check in the back again, when will it be in, what time does the truck come?" All over some thing she didn't even know she wanted until the weekly ad came out and told her to want it. Jodie just stood there, not crying though, and apologized over and over, like we were told to do, waiting on the manager who would come and apologize some more, basically until the customer had enough or maybe was given enough. Man, some of them people would stick around like a piece of gristle between your teeth. We all learned the look, the minimum wage stare, the look that pleads with the customer to please just give up because we can't fix it, but we won't care about not fixing it. There was nothing else we could do; Bullseye brought the shit but didn't give us a plunger. In return, the customer can say just about anything to us. Bullseye values its guests, so much that for a $4.99 purchase they can treat us this way. Self-respect goes cheap in Aisle 38.

Most of us were just trying to make a little money. But some people were spayed. They'd been yelled at too many times, or were too afraid of losing their jobs. They were broke. People—and dogs—don't get like that quickly; it has to build up on them, or tear down on them, like erosion, one thing after another nudging them deeper into it. Then one day, if the supervisor told them by mistake to hang a sign upside down, they'd do it, more afraid of contradicting the boss than making an obvious mistake. You'd see them rushing in like twenty minutes early to stand next to that clock so they wouldn't be late. One associate broke down in tears when she accidentally dropped something, afraid she'd get fired on the spot for it. They all walked around like the floor was all stray cat tails, step on one and set off all the cats screaming. It was a shitty way to live as an adult, your only incentive to doing good work being they'd let you keep a job that made you hate yourself for another day.

Fear controlled a lot of us, but there was something worse I think. Like with Muley and those sadistic bastard football coaches, some guys at Bullseye just didn't get it. They really seemed to believe this shit about customer love and working harder. Most of us understood we had to pay it lip service around the managers, and they mostly knew they had to say it back at us. Both sides were looking the other way, a lot like whores and their customers saying "I love you" to each other I guess. But then there'd be a guy who just lived it, like a religious convert. He had a bunch of pins and buttons on his name tag lanyard, saying shit like YOU'RE MY NUMBER ONE CUSTOMER! And if someone said thank you for something, he'd say, "It was my pleasure to provide you with five-star service!" like he even knew what the hell that meant. I didn't.

In the break room I heard one valued associate say to another, "Man, I'm your friend, so I gotta tell you, you smell."

Then the other associate said back, "I know, I ain't had a shower for a few days. No hot water at my place 'til I can pay the gas bill."

"We're six days away from the next pay day."

"I know. I talked to my old guidance counselor and he's gonna let me sneak into the high school and shower there."

That associate got fired the next week for stealing food, other associates' lunches in the break room refrigerator.

But most everybody found their way. It was all about money, surviving, providing, like with Jodie and her two kids and no boyfriend. Jodie wasn't so unique; half of all single-parent families live in poverty. Our life at Bullseye wasn't unique. Me and Jodie were actually part of a trend. Look at Wal-Mart. I read somewhere they had revenue bigger than 170 different countries, including some of the Arab countries that have oil. Hell, Wal-Mart has more than two million employees, so if Wal-Mart was an army, it would be the largest military on the planet behind China. Wal-Mart is the largest private employer in the U.S.

Jodie did ask me to move in with her. Her apartment was a mess. Junk from Bullseye, stuff from the used furniture store, paintings of Jesus in gold frames, a mix of Goodwill and pictures I'd seen of Graceland. I spent a few nights, but I couldn't handle the kids tryin' to get me to answer to "daddy, daddy, daddy." She was always tryin' to set up these domestic scenes with me and the kids, putting one of them on the floor with me piling up blocks, saying, "Want to grow up and work at Bullseye like Mommy and Uncle Earl?" while the other banged a spoon on the table for attention until I thought I'd go fucking nuts. Then one night in bed we was just lying there and she pulled my hand over to her warm belly and said, "Imagine one for us kicking inside." I could, and then saying no was as simple in the doing as it was long-standing in the consequence. One time earlier when she was late and before we knew it was a false alarm, I was secretly ready to force myself to stay, hearing of all things Angie's voice in my head telling me not to do to Jodie what everyone else was doing to me.

As for them kids, the one was always trying to slide into bed with us, and the other, he never said much at all, just watched TV in a kind of creepy way. I had no idea how to be a real father to them. I would have loved to push my own kids on the swings, saying, "back and a-wwwway" while they laughed. But I was too poor to do it. Hell, my mom served portions, and threw away portions, that would have fed Fred Flintstone. I knew these kids was going to grow up never having enough now, meaning they would never be satisfied, never really full, later on. A lot like my dad's foreman, Depression Kid—he kept old aluminum foil and shopping bags folded in the basement, never threw out anything, used to lick the dinner plates clean in the kitchen when he thought nobody was looking. No matter what he achieved, Eagle Scout, college degree, captain's rank, he could never rest. Nothing could ever be enough.

Before I gave up, there was a potential, a white shirt maybe a little dirty, but with another good washing left in it to carry it into tomorrow. I had known prosperity, I had a place, at least in theory, I could bounce back to. Not these kids. They are never going to know where back is. They ain't never gonna trust no one, never gonna trust nothing they didn't put down with their own hand. When I was little, we all wanted to be astronauts. What do they have to grow up to be? To work at Bullseye? Jodie and those boys wanted me to give them some kind of a future when I couldn't see down the road for myself, never mind for three other already wounded people. She said "I love you" to me a couple of times, but we both knew it wasn't love or lust— maybe just comfort, or something practical. If they were lies, and you wanted to choose to believe them, then there wasn't no sin. Sometimes that's all you can expect, and sometimes that's enough.

Still, me and Jodie got along well even just as friends, and we both were hoping to get ahead some now that we had steady part-time work at Bullseye. We thought of ways we could help each other. One day her kids were sick and she didn't want to leave them home alone, so she brought them in to work. She told them to stay in the toy aisle all day looking at things, pretending like they could buy them, and me and Jodie took turns quietly checking on them until quitting time. Some cough-soothing syrup went missing that day too between my picking and Pharmacy's filling. That day of all days Jodie got asked again to work through her break, so I had to feed them sick kids Ho-Ho's and red pop for lunch, which probably made them feel better than me overall.

Our biggest attempt at trying to help each other was after Jodie transferred to sporting goods and one day told me how customers were always asking her for Ace bandages and white tape and stuff. That all was kept over in Pharmacy. Bullseye told us our guests were the most important product, and had Rule Number 3 that if a guest asked for something somewhere else in the store you couldn't just say, "Sure, over in Aisle Seven," but you had to walk them there as a courtesy and wait to see if they found what they were looking for or needed additional guest service interaction. Jodie said the problem was so many people kept asking for athletic tape that she was walking a lot and her team manager, Ephraim, was on her ass for not being at her station near the bowling items. She told Ephraim about the athletic tape taking her away, but he said something about her needing to learn to work smarter not harder, which did not seem to help, because the athletic tape was still not where customers were asking for it. Having to actually talk to the customers, we came to understand, was the weak link in the chain of efficiently transferring money from them to Bullseye.

"So Earl," Jodie said, sharing a Twinkie on break, "I know how we can get ahead here. We can do this thing called innovation Ephraim told us about at the last team-building meeting. He said we have to be ahead of our customers' needs to succeed in this market. So, here's my plan. You pick me some athletic bandages and tape, just a few at first, and put them in my tub instead of Pharmacy. I'll have the new things set up all nice near my station, and when Ephraim comes by I'll show them off. We'll get promoted maybe. For sure win that 'Catch Us Doing Our Best' prize."

I think it was only because firing two valued teammates at the same time would've made Steve and Ephraim look bad, or because they couldn't figure out a way to blame it on one another, that we didn't get thrown out that day. Ephraim was a cooler Team Leader, explaining to Jodie about unit stock control, location sales metrics, and how important it was that each Bullseye store maintain its unique identical layout. Steve just told me never to do anything that wasn't on the pick sheet again, or he'd call security and have me walked out. He also secretly tagged me as "IE" on my performance review, ineligible for rehire it meant, which I only found out later after I was laid off and trying to use Bullseye as a reference for Taco Bell. Jodie got reassigned to the children's section, which everyone hated because it was where the most shoplifting took place and she was worried about having to see one of her mom friends doing it. Her first task was to put out only one shoe of a pair on display, keep the other one in the back until someone paid, to discourage people from stealing 'cause they couldn't get the set. After customers just started stealing any old right shoe to go with any left shoe on the rack, Jodie had to redo it so there were only left shoes on display.

I got put on busing tables at the Food Courtyard. Because the waitresses were supposed to share tips with us bus boys, the

Bullseye family was not legally required to pay minimum wage, so I got three bucks less an hour than before. That most sales in the Courtyard were like four dollars for coffee and a sandwich, and the average tip thirty cents, and only about half the waitresses would share half the time anyway, it wasn't the best. Throw some peanuts and watch the monkey dance. Sometimes though I was quicker and could slide the change off the table into my bus tray along with the dishes and cheat those bitches back. Most of the customers were daytime moms desperate for some little bit of adult human contact. You'd think there'd be a million stories in a place like this, but there's only one. Even the food was gonna depress you; big colorful posters of perfect rounded burgers and stuffed sandwiches made by artists, and then we serve you a warmed over flat thing.

One day I recognized one of the customers.

"Earl, is that you? I haven't seen you since when, high school?"

"Yeah, hi, how you been?"

"Great. Just home from the city for a few days to see the folks, you know. Had to pick up a few things and figured I'd grab a bite. You wanna sit down?"

"I work here."

"Oh, well, yeah, cool, so this is what you do?"

"I'll just get someone to take your order."

At one point to fix the economy we were gonna have legalized gambling and build a casino in Reeve, but it turned out anybody who'd want to gamble around here didn't have enough money to gamble it away. Then for a while the big hope was for a German car factory to locate in our part of Ohio. It was in all

134

the news. At one point cars were pretty much made in Detroit, all around that Greenfield Village museum we took the field trip to in high school. Somehow we got from there to here, where cars are made by foreign companies and Detroit looks like Dresden after WWII and Dresden looks like Detroit before WWII. Still, if our state could give the Germans enough of our tax money as an incentive, and enough work visas for their most skilled workers and managers to come over from Germany, they'd build cars to sell us here in Ohio and we'd have some more jobs that the Germans didn't get, which was a lot like stealing tips. I noticed some foreigners in nice clothes come in to the food court now and then, along with our politicians who were offering those incentives. I'd listen in on them while I was wiping things up, hoping to get the inside track on when those jobs would come.

"Mr. Mayor, we thank you for your hospitality. Our friend here from your governor's office has taken us around to so many of your rustic small towns. I must say, Ohio is quite beautiful."

"We do like it here Manfred—may I call you that? But of course in addition to being so pretty a countryside, we have a lot of hard-working Americans anxious to get started."

"And that, if I may be blunt Mr. Mayor, is our concern. The tax breaks are generous, and your promise of a better highway to allow us to ship parts from Munich via the Columbus airport is important. What worries us, frankly, are the workers. Our motorcars are complex machines, and our quality is our brand. Can your people meet our standards, at our price?"

"These are good people, Manfred. Salt of the earth."

"Mr. Mayor, allow me to tell you a true story. Apple had redesigned their iPhone's display literally at the last minute. New screens began arriving at the assembly plant in China near midnight the day before the units were to ship. A foreman roused 8,000 workers inside the company's dormitories, gave them each a hard biscuit and a cup of tea and sent them into the factory for work. Within thirty minutes of being woken, they started a twelve-hour shift fitting displays without a break to meet Apple's deadline. Can your workers do that? Do they have those kinds of skills? Perhaps, of course, we would serve coffee instead of tea here. A little joke, yes?"

"Um, well, Manfred, I just don't know. I mean, we have laws here, about people being able to sleep and how long they can work."

"In my China factories I do not even by law have to allow workers breaks for water or sanitation. We do find limited meals are necessary for productivity. Those are the skills I need. Can your people provide them?"

"Manfred, really, those aren't skills, getting out of bed to work in the middle of the night, twelve-hour shifts. You can't bully your workers. Can you? What you're talking is more like, well, I don't know, more like you need farm animals than people."

"Ha yes, Mr. Mayor. I understand your joke in English. We indeed have such a saying in German as well. You are funny, but in North Carolina they are offering us the incentive of using prison labor if we locate the plant there, only a few of your pennies an hour. I do think it would cost more to feed farm animals. That is my joke to you. But yes, yes, of course I understand. I have opened factories for our company all over the world, and I have heard the same thing in Shenzhen and in Chennai. In the end, there I have found workers at our price point, in our needed quantity, with the skills we require, despite these so-called 'laws.' It is flexibility those places offer me. Of course, your people do speak good English, and that is a plus for us. But can you guarantee me that they'll work to our standards? Can you assure me for example that there will not be a union here to disrupt our labor price calculations?"

"Well, on the quality, sure, they'll do it, of course. And now, you know I can't control the thing about the union here—"

"Mr. Mayor, again, we are in your country and I am happy to follow your custom of direct speech. My company needs a North American facility, but our margins are tight. I can drop this plant across the border in Mexico as easily as I can drop it here. You will please think about that. Meantime, allow me to think over what you have said, maybe take a closer look at your labor pool, 'size them up,' I think you say in English, no?"

I had heard about this and it wasn't just in China. In Mississippi, Nissan claims never to have laid anyone off at their car plant. That's because more than a quarter of their workers are employed by temp agencies and laid off at will, but by the temp agency, not Nissan, still with its clean hands. The workers say in eight years they have never seen a temp promoted to regular. FastEx Ground classifies thousands of drivers as independent contractors, so they get no benefits. Those drivers have to pay for their own gas, and rent their trucks. Still having to buy from the company store.

I did get one thing outta the Germans. For a while one of them had his wife staying with him in town, sort of checking us out I guess to see if their German kids could grow up here. She hired me under the table to do some yard work, cleaning gutters and painting a bit, saying even their rented place wasn't right for her, as she had come from Europe. Whatever, I made a few bucks, she gave me coffee and we actually got to know each other a little while I was working. One day she invited me inside to move some stuff and, you know it, like in them videos, we ended up in bed. She never called me back, but she slipped me a sweet fifty that day, mumbling how it wasn't much in real Euros anyway, so there's your American worker, job done right.

Back at Bullseye things didn't go as smoothly. It wasn't anything I did, but they hired some kid to bus tables and I got sent back to my old job, though I always wondered if any of the waitresses secretly caught me stealing their nickels and dimes off the tables. One of them could have seen me at the bowling alley buying beer with handfuls of change maybe. Anyway, the second time around the picking and stocking job didn't last too long. Steve the Team Leader explained one day that Bullseye had innovated a new warehousing system that centralized item distribution in such a way that goods came to our store already sorted into tubs. Instead of me breaking down a big box of razors or toothpaste into tubs for Pharmacy and tubs for Grocery, it was done centrally somewhere else by someone else. The people who used to just have to pick up their filled tubs from me were redefined so that they now went into the big truck directly and lifted out their pre-filled tubs. They could skip their own bar code reading part, and so Steve laid off three of those people for efficiency, too. Steve did thank me very nicely for my contributions to the Bullseye family and took my blue vest. At first I was so mad I wanted to burn down the building and bayonet the survivors, but Steve said he hoped I would leave without a fuss. I did. I guess in the end I had precious little fuss left in me.

BEING UNEMPLOYED AGAIN meant lots of time on my hands. When it was too hot or too cold outside and I had a few bucks in my jeans, I liked to spend time in the new coffee shop at the strip mall here in Reeve. I'd buy a cup, drink some, then load it up with sugar and milk. Drink some more, slowly, reload with sugar and milk, and keep doing it until it was just milk or I got caught. The owners were Koreans and would take the milk container in right after the morning rush, but when one of the few local staff was at the counter (those Korean families were only so big and could only cover so many hours no matter how greedy they was, plus I think they liked the idea of us havin' to work for them), I could do that milk thing all afternoon.

The other thing I liked about the coffee shop was the Korean girls that would come in for bubble tea, the kind that requires that big-ass straw. I tried one of those straws on my coffee once, but it made me drink too fast. Not a working man's straw. The girls were all young and pretty, maybe a little too much makeup at nine in the morning sometimes, but everybody had to make a living. I tried to chat a few of them up, but they either didn't speak English or didn't see the point in talking with a guy who obviously had no play money. Most of them worked at that club without windows, and most of the customers going in and out were Koreans too, dropping money as if they were allergic to it. I doubt too many of Reeve's other citizens could afford an import.

I did have some hope for this one woman who seemed to linger a bit longer than most of them. She might have been a little older, hard to tell age exactly with Orientals, but she'd sit outside and smoke while her friends would grab their tea and head right back to work. I wasn't sure what was the right way to approach her, but after some clumsy eye contact and some spilled coffee trying to bump into her accidentally twice at the door, we did get to talking. Spoke good English although without ever satisfying the letters R and L, which I kinda got used to. At first it was mostly hello and good morning, but once she realized I wasn't angling for anything, we'd talk while she smoked and got to know one another.

Kim, my angel of the strip mall.

Man, she was a whole story in a sigh. I always wanted to know why she did what she did, you know, her job. I especially wanted to know if she had a boyfriend or whatever they called it over in Korea. She is probably too busy to get on the bus with me right now, but I remembered her none the less.

"Why my job any different than yours?" Kim asked me. "I saw that movie, 'greed is good.' I wanna make my money."

It helped that day that I had had a couple of eye-openers for breakfast out of that half-finished bottle of Everclear from last night's therapy. Okay, maybe I drank half the damn bottle before breakfast.

"Kim, I'm sorta embarrassed to ask, but—"

"Little brother Earl, I have sex with strangers for money. I don't embarrass."

Kim didn't get embarrassed. She just said stuff. Not like Reeve girls.

"Okay, you, you know, sell your—"

"Kitty. That's what I got, that's what I sell."

"Aren't you—"

"Oh cut the shit. You no virgin, and I'm not either. We all do what we have to do. It's a job. I'm in business, taking as much as I can from them and giving as little as I can get away with. I want to be dirty rich, no, you say filthy rich, same thing. I give them with my kitty, not my brain. I no there. Maybe you look and see him naked, I look and see his wallet on the dresser. If he on top of me, I look up at my nails and think about what polish color is best. You, boy friend Earl, what'd you do last week for money?"

"Some guy hired me, two bucks an hour, though he short-changed me on the last twenty minutes, to pick up construction crap and throw it in a Dumpster."

"And you used your body, used your muscles, yeah? Got all sweaty? Pretended to be enthused about some shitty work?"

"I get it Kim, but I ain't no whore. I work for my money, hard work."

"Me too baby. I also ain't no whore. It no different. You selling your body, I selling mine. Guys who pay me, they selling something somewhere else to make their money. Anyway, look at them. I use their sad, weak parts. They more pathetic than me 'cause they lying to they wives and they lying to themselves. Even you. You'd fuck me Earl, if you had the money. I let you, if you had the money, but nothing for free little boy. You pay for coffee, you pay for me. And I saw you stealing the milk too. You in love with all those little high school chicks you screwed?"

"No. Course not."

"And they no in love with you, yeah?"

"Right, but we both were wanting, so it was okay."

"Yeah, me too. He want to do me for sex, and I want to do him for dollar. Different reason, but the same in the end. Everybody wants something, that's what money is for, stupid boy Earl."

"But ain't you ashamed or something?"

"You made few bucks an hour. I could do that at a nail salon with your mother my customer, sure, but I can pull in fifty, sixty, maybe a hundred an hour with the right guy and my kitty."

So I sorta understood that you could imagine you still owned something you'd sold, at least until you ended up sleeping in a bath tub hoping one of the seven guys a night would leave a few bucks on your sticky belly after he left. See, I knew my way around this. There was a bar called The Promised Land run mostly for Mexicans, but in the back was another room where they said they told fortunes. You paid up at the bar for a palm reading, they had a sign and all, and went back in. It was cheap, not classy like I imagined Kim's place, designed more for the Mexican day workers, but they'd service anyone. It was just dark and shadows and then some chiquita would reach out and take your hand and lead you off to a cot without sheets. It smelled like Clorox and sweat. It was quick and sad, not even fast food. Sometimes I'd be more lonely than the other thing, but them girls didn't speak English, not like Kim. They'd say "okay, okay" to whatever you said, but even in the dark you could see there were no smiles. I guess it was fair, 'cause I wasn't smiling either. In the end, paying for sex was mostly about not being alone.

They didn't like to kiss, but would let you sorta do it if pushing back was harder than giving in. Every time you'd taste cigarettes and gum. Kinda odd, a girl who'd suck you off wouldn't kiss you back, but that really told the story if you could understand the language. When it was done she'd hand you a baby wipe in the dark and you'd walk out still alone. After a while when fucking was, well, just fucking, you started to forget how it could be anything else. It was just appetite, and we were all embarrassed to be hungry, but we had to eat. Funny thing, the cops closed the bar down because getting fucked for money was illegal. I then recognized two of the girls working in Bullseye just the next week when I went in for my last paycheck. Small world.

I was talking some more to Kim.

"So, they just walk in and you guys, what? Just fall on the floor?"

"You an idiot. Gimme that lighter, I wanna smoke before I go back. They come in, pay sixty dollars to the house. Some old whore Mama who married one of the gangsters takes the money from them and passes them back to me or one of the other girls. If Mama likes you, she'll throw the rich-looking ones your way. To make Mama like you, you gotta kick back to her some of your tips. She gotta turn over her money to the gangsters, or they'll beat her up or worse, stop sending her fresh kitty like me. A whole club full of cheap street meat mean no customers come back. She bitch. Right, or you say 'she a bitch'? Don't matter, everybody screwing everybody."

"So the guy get passed to me, and I size him up. He know the game? He know the price? If he's new, I try to pull as much as I can up front. But most of the guys know it all, so I gotta play them. I worry he might want to change girls too, maybe I not pretty enough or my tits too small or remind him of his wife, so right away I take his pants off. He no gonna run out naked. On the table, we start massage. I tease him. The more he lay there thinking about fucking me, the more money I gonna make. I start out behind, owing Mama her off-the-book tip, plus I owe the house another twenty bucks for towel fee. They making all the money, man. I work the guy all over his back, teasing underneath, making sure he not bored. Mama told him the house fee was for an hour, and if he finish too fast he thinks he got cheated or I have to talk to him to fill time. An hour is at least forty-five minutes now days. Anyway, him on his stomach longer mean I don't have to see his face for more time."

"I turn him over. If he not hard, I get him happy before I ask for the money. I ask for $200. He knows that's a joke, and I see what he really will pay. Or maybe he no understand, and I get my money. Whatever he wants, when he asks what it cost, I just say 'more.' One way is as much trouble as the next. Most of them finish quickly, or I tell them to hurry up. 'Oh, you so big. Oh, you turn me on baby. Oh, you make me come, honey.' I don't mean it, and he don't believe it, but we playing the game. He probably starting to think of his wife and feel guilty anyway, and then he never finish. I hate that, feels like I am doing hand laundry in the sink. He finish, he pay, and he leave. I make more now anyway, with my fake boobs. Invest in yourself baby. These two cost me five hundred."

As she said that, I came to realize that Kim was a woman made of many products, a whole arsenal of creams and lotions, nail enamels, makeup and hair color, so it wasn't out of place that other parts of her came from a store too. What was real and what was made up seemed to matter little when you were making money. Fooling customers was part of the process, and they readily participated. Kim was nothing if not consistent.

"Ain't you afraid of the cops around here?"

"Nah, Mama usually know all the cops, not like those stupid Mexicans. She send cops back same as anyone, but they no have to tip, it free for them. Cost of doing business, jerking off a cop once in a while. Ha, ha, stupid Earl, maybe you try it once, jerk off the cop out there in your parking lot and he leave you alone too."

On the bus I kept seeing that one Korean kid, the only person riding the bus I didn't recognize, so I just nicknamed him "Tom" 'cause it was easy to remember. I worried who he was, thinking I must have known the kid from around the coffee shop, or somewhere at this strip mall. There were enough Koreans around for sure, but I could not place the one on the bus. He wasn't the kid that got beat up in the parking lot a while back, this one was even younger. I thought it might have to do with Kim, so I got my courage up to ask.

"You aren't worried about, you know, a baby? Havin' sex with all them men?"

"Yeah, I have a baby, had, a baby somewhere. Couldn't afford to keep her, too expensive and getting in the way of my work. Got to cut expenses, cut overhead, cut personnel, you know. Baby not efficient, so I took her to Christian orphanage.

That's economics. Usually it 'no glove, no love,' but some guys pay me double for no condom. If I wanna make money, gotta have business risk."

"Do they know you, see you outside work? You know, like your boyfriend?"

"No way. You stupid. I can't afford a boyfriend, they want free sex. I tell customers my nickname is 'Money,' or they call me whatever name they like, like owning a dog, they get to pick it. It don't matter to me. I forget their names even before the smell of their cum leave my room. You don't get it Earl. They my customers. They buy something from me, pay and leave. We say 'in, up, off, out,' like we practicing English verbs. I never see them outside. You have more of a relationship with the counter guy at the coffee shop you buy from? It just sex, baby. I gotta make it now, while I got my looks. My time is short."

Kim wasn't just some mousetrap. I sorta had feelings for her by this time.

"I never met a woman like you. You're not afraid of sex, you can talk about it. It's effortless with you. Maybe it's the booze talking now, but I think I love you Kim."

"Do you?"

"Kim, I've never met someone like you. I really think I love you."

"Guys I do for money tell me that all the time. Love you, love you, love you baby."

"Whattaya say back?"

"I say 'I love you too,' because they tip more that way. Just business, like 'Have a nice day!' Makes people feel good."

"But you don't mean it?"

"Have a nice day? Sure I do. You an asshole."

"You know what I'm asking, Kim."

"I don't have to mean 'I love you,' I just have to say it. Just words."

"I never meant to fall in love with you, Kim."

"Yeah, I love you too."

One time I ran into Kim at the coffee shop after dark, and she asked me to walk her back to work. She entered through the back door. Door didn't have any handle on the outside, as if announcing clearly I was not welcome; somebody had to push it open for you from the inside. Kim would yell something in Korean, and Mama or one of the others would open it, always with a scowl for me. Mama was rough on all the edges, called everyone "Honey" in a voice like she stopped smoking cigarettes and just chewed on them, eye makeup that looked like it hadn't been pried outta her wrinkles in years. Breath that would peel paint, good paint. Ugly, sorta like forage the deers wouldn't eat until the end of winter even if they was hungry. Smelled of garbage out back there, greasy trash from the fast-food places next door. The big smell came from inside the club however, a storm when the door opened, a flood of perfume and disinfectant, the two not getting along, competing with each other for ownership of your nose. After walking Kim over two or three more times, she'd say if it looked like a slow night, and she'd prop the back door open and we'd talk. She slam it shut quick when Mama called, and I'd sometimes hang out, waiting for that forty five minute hour to be up for the customer and she'd open up and we'd talk more. Sometimes she'd hand me some soda or something from inside, when the customer wouldn't take the drink she was supposed to offer him as a signal it was time for him to get out.

One night I had my first ever hit of speed from Kim. Mama handed out little red and blue pills so the girls would work longer hours, and Kim said if she took two or three or four or eight her head spun and the time passed more quickly. Kim looked tired without the speed, but when I said something she'd laugh at me and say, "I don't even open my eyes until after midnight." Some nights Mama laid out lines of the new, cheap coke coming into town to perk up her girls. Hours were pretty rough for Kim at the club, basically stay on as long as customers were coming, but it was her job and she had a work ethic. I just hung out for something to do.

By now I was used to finding myself in a place without a really specific reason for being there. Sometimes in the dark I'd see people in the Dumpsters looking for food or whatever. I don't think they lived there, just came to eat, like them animals in nature documentaries coming to the water hole. When I was a kid, the places in Reeve where you could go at night to do technically illegal but really just wayward stuff like climbing the water tower, or pulling off some road to make out, were limited. Desire and interest were there, but usually without opportunity; you didn't want someone to tell your mom the next day that they'd seen the family car parked behind some store. In those days, you couldn't find a place like this, back of a strip mall, that was public enough no one knew you but still private enough that you could do whatever you wanted.

I started noticing the same couple of cars from time to time, one maroon, a big old LTD, and the other light green, I think, a righteous Camaro for sure. All Detroit iron, when that mattered. They'd pull up nose-to-tail, and the drivers would exchange something. Had to be drugs. Like I said, we had weed in Reeve forever, but the speed and shit Kim took was new, kinda fighting for turf with the home-made meth. Meth was a local product, but this new stuff was factory-made, maybe another import pushing out an American product. I didn't know much about drug deals, but it seemed odd that they always used the same place, since that'd make it easier to get caught. Once, when they came a bit earlier and it was still a little light, I thought I recognized one of the guys in the Camaro from high school. I waited for the other car to pull away and shouted his name. No response, so I walked outta the shadows a bit so he could see me, sayin' the kid's name again, kind of pleased to recognize someone. He tore away, and I didn't think anything of it until about ten minutes later two cops roll up. I was scared, trying hard to think of what to say, thinking they wanted me to rat out what was going on. The one cop stayed near the car and the other got up in my face.

"What're you doing here, son?"

"Just lookin' for a place to stand, sir."

"You seen anything tonight?"

"Officer, just some cars driving through."

"Recognize anybody? Seen anyone you know?"

"No sir." I saw he had his billy club out of the sling.

"Then why'd you shout out a boy's name and start on down?"

They must have been watching from somewhere.

"What's that, officer? No sir, wasn't me." I was really worried now, and hoping like hell the door wouldn't swing open and get Kim mixed into this mess. I was sort of mumbling to buy time, my brain trying to catch on the right thing to say when the cop interrupted me.

"Well little boy, listen up close. Nothing here is your business. You don't see nothing. You don't call out no names. Them people got friends, and you fucking don't."

It was just in between the words "fucking" and "don't" that he snapped that billy club right into my balls, kind of a hard flick that spiraled me back and made everything turn all purple. The cop gave me a sort of friendly shove so that I landed on my ass.

"Understand now? Hard times around here, dickhead. We all gotta do what we need to get by, just like that slope bitch of yours inside. You look familiar—have I busted you before? Anyways, you're a local kid I can tell or I'd kick your ass back into last week to make my point clearer. Around here we gotta take care of our own. You don't see nothing, you keep your mouth shut. Ain't nobody paying you to watch this go down, and we ain't gonna tolerate you getting into what we're doing, or my partner and I'll be liking you on some sort of vagrancy charge or worse. Maybe pop your ass and find some coke on you, know what I mean? Just spend your time with your whore and everything will work out for all of us."

The cop stepped back and reslung his billy.

"I don't want to do this again, I really fucking don't. You know things are messed up—so learn fast and don't go pissing in someone's lunch box."

It wasn't over. In a decent world that would have been the end of that day. I would have walked home, had some dinner, maybe dessert. Instead I noticed another guy walking towards me. Wasn't a cop. This used to not be a problem in Reeve but these days you had to be on your guard. It was dark, nobody paying for new streetlights in this part of the town, and before I could make him out he asked me for change. He crinkled up a plastic bag, distracting me, but I realized there his voice was in the old part of me.

"Muley?"

"Who's that? I don't want no trouble mister, just some spare change if you got it."

"Muley, that you? It's me, Earl."

"Earl?" We stepped closer now, less like two dogs sniffing each other out.

"Where you been, man?"

"Where I been? Shit Muley, you was the one joined the Army and been gone. How you been?"

"I been okay enough. Home for a while, just never looked you up right I guess. Looked for a job first instead, but they wasn't hiring. Plenty of people willing to slap my back 'cause I was a soldier but nobody gave me a job. I called your house once, but your dad said you moved out somewheres."

"That sucks man, but it's the same for all of us, no fucking work. What the hell is that you got there? Smells like fucking paint."

"You want some? Since I been back I started in on this shit, huffin' until I forget why I started it. Can't taste food no more neither. Weird, huh? But bein' on the paint is way-shit cheaper

151

than beer, and a seriously fucked up buzz. Ain't illegal either, I think. Jest paint." He had a cigarette tucked behind his ear, and I was hoping he'd not try and light it around those spray cans.

"Earl, you watched that new Star Wars? Kinda sucks, man."

"Muley, I seen some bad shit tonight, real bad."

"Earl, we all seen bad shit. It's the way it is now."

"Muley, we're all grown up, man."

"Then I wish I could grow back down."

We stopped talking for a moment. I kept trying to meet Muley's eyes, but he kept looking away. Only sound was him rattling the goddamn little glass ball inside the paint can.

"Fuck man, that paint shit'll mess you up."

"Too late Earl, I'm already messed up. Looks like you is too, old friend. This is where we are now."

KIM'S MOM HAD been in her same business back in Seoul, and Kim grew up thinking her dad might have been an American soldier because they were the ones most often in line, saying "Hey little girl, how's your mama tonight? I want a blow job."

"You know, Kim, my old man always talked about all the fun he had in Korea, just booze and broads, like any American soldier overseas, I guess. You know how it is."

"Yeah, I know dumb fuck boy Earl. My mama was a broad like you say."

"You really think your old man might have been an American?"

"American, French, Italian, they were United Nations."

"You never knew your dad?"

"I saw him every night lined up outside my mother's door."

"Things weren't so good between me and my dad either. Some days I thought my crime was just being born."

"Yeah, you tell me about it puppy dog Earl."

Kim's mom I guess really didn't know who, and Kim said that back then abortions were rare in Korea, legal abortions almost unheard of. Her mom was a Christian anyway, so when she got pregnant she dropped out of the work for a while. Usually such babies ended up in one of Korea's many, many orphanages to be adopted by naive but well-meaning Americans, going from place to place like they was shopping for a puppy, Kim said. They never knew most of those cute babies were whore spawn. Kim's mom kept her for her own reasons. She said one day an American missionary convinced her mom to take her to the U.S. embassy and claim her father was a soldier, thinking maybe some money might come of it. Her mom had saved a handful of letters from some random dumbass GI from Oklahoma who thought he fell in love with the first woman to give him head, and she showed those to the embassy guy as proof. The embassy guy laughed at her, having seen his share of whores with babies at his interview window before, and told her to come back with a notarized Affidavit of Support with original signature in black ink only from the father. U.S. law covered the GIs well, saying the baby wasn't an American if born out of wedlock without that Affidavit; otherwise, the baby was just another Korean slut's kid, whether she had red hair, white skin and blue eyes or the freaking Star Spangled Banner tattooed under the diaper. Same as in Vietnam, Taiwan, and everywhere else, I heard. Kim's mom spent three nights' wages on a terrible fake Affidavit she bought off the street in Namdemun market, and that didn't even get her past the guard at the embassy gate, it was so bad.

Jobs were hard to find in Korea then for people without education, especially women. So coming to America was about the same as us packing up and driving to California or Alaska for a new life. Working inside the Korean community was about it, and even that required moving further and further down the ladder sometimes until you ended up in a club without windows in a strip mall in Reeve. Still, it was a go-go economy, we were told on the news, and making money was good in and of itself, no matter what you did for it. Selling stocks, selling your kitty, wasn't it all about the same? Kim believed so. I became sort of convinced she was right, and maybe a little jealous that I had nothing like that to sell myself.

Me and Kim were talking as usual at that back door between customers, and she seemed more wound up than other nights, sayin' things a mile a minute, smoking one cig after another. I tried to cheer her up a bit, told her a joke I remembered, said that I really felt that I knew her now.

"Be quiet child boy Earl. You know nothing about me."

"Oh yeah? Tell me something you think I don't know about you Kim. One thing, go ahead."

"My whole life I never got to kiss anyone I liked."

WE BOTH HEARD Mama shouting "guest, guest," and Kim went back inside quickly, closing the door and turning up her music. I don't know if she cranked the tunes for her customer or not, but

I wanted to believe it was for me, that she didn't want me to be able to hear what went on. I usually just zoned out at this point, relaxing, but there was a noise, a loud noise, from inside. This was the wrong kind of sound, somebody falling, and I pulled at the edges of the door with my fingernails trying to get it open, hoping Kim hadn't slid the bolt lock shut from the inside. My muscles weren't what they used to be, lack of work and exercise, and I tore the tip of my finger open on a sliver of exposed steel trying to pry that goddamn door open. Blood ran down the door, and I pulled my hand back and sucked at the wound. Hurt almost as much as when I messed up my ankle back in high school. I went back at the door, got it open enough to get my hand around the edge, and saw Mama bent over Kim, with some guy pulling on his pants as he pushed past me into the darkness. Hard almond eyes were too wide and didn't blink, light drained from them, and she had spit up the little dough balls from the bottom of her last bubble tea. Some blood. I saw Kim naked for the first time, but not in a good way, cum sliding down her leg even as she lay there. Mama was feeling for a pulse at Kim's wrist, saying too many blues and too many reds for a girl her size in one night. I tried to get closer, maybe just to wipe her off for Christ's sake, but Mama snarled at me like Satan's alley cat. "Go away goddamn you, and don't say nothing," she hissed, "this ain't your business." She turned back to Kim, knowing that as sure as if I had seen the Devil himself, I would turn away and never say a thing.

I never did. Nothing about me was ever completely the same, though. I maybe could've done something, I don't know, called for help or something, but I didn't. I ain't saying this absolves me of all I didn't do with my life later on, just know there was more to it than drink and laziness.

Sermon on the Mount

"JESUS, IS THAT you? Casey, is that you getting on this bus?"

"Yeah man, it's me. Sometimes I get on the bus too."

Casey slid into the seat next to me, smiling that little crooked smile that favored his few missing teeth. He looked older, but hell, Casey always looked older, like he was carrying something around that had gotten heavy.

"Earl."

"Casey."

"Been on this bus long?"

"Jesus, Casey, I ain't seen you in, what, years? How you been? What you been doing? That's all you got to say to me, 'Been on this bus long?' Yeah, I been on this freaking bus forever man, my whole life. Casey, it's really good to see you."

"Same here Earl."

"So what you been doing Casey since I last seen you?"

"Long story, Earl, long story, but you first man. You doing okay?"

Casey knew, he must have. He always seemed to hear more than was said anyway. But I told him, about how on and off for the past year or so I had been living in my car. No work, no job, and before you know it, you're living in your car and glad to have it. Like so many things, it starts easy enough, failing to make the rent and moving into a day-by-day place, a room with a hot plate burner, down the hall from some whores aspiring to become crack heads, then slipping again and taking to sleeping in your car every couple of nights to save a little money. Bitch in the summer, worse in the winter, but in between, with the right kinda seats, it wasn't so bad. Couple nights in, couple out, stretch the money a bit while staying pretty clean. But what you don't see is what other people see. Go too many days without a shower, wash your clothes too many times in a motel sink, and you start to look like what you didn't realize you'd become— homeless—your new history like dirt accumulating on you, you smelling like water broccoli has been boiled in.

You can in fact tell a lot about a homeless guy based on how clean he is, like counting tree rings. There's the newbies, then the 'tweens like me on the down slide, and then the zombie homeless, more filth than man, covered in street gravy. The whole homeless ecosystem. When the new guys rubbed their eyes, they made black spots like raccoons. When the old timers rubbed their eyes, they made clean spots. Me? I was filthy enough that some days I worried someone would write WASH ME in the dirt on my ass.

At first it was easier. Look around one of those coffee shops the next time you're downtown and try and spot the homeless and semi-homeless, 'cause we're there, payin' for coffee with change. Sometimes I'd just grab an empty cup from the trash outside, because if I got five bucks for a drink, it ain't gonna be a mocha grande. Fill a table and, when I was cleaner, lean over and make some excuse to use someone's phone or computer to look for work on Craigslist, because everything found a new home on-line and without devices you couldn't get very far. People like me fill out applications, we don't have resumes, and few businesses'll let you do anything on paper anymore.

And with a job application, don't write down the shelter address if you're staying at one, in case they know it, or nowadays, Google it. Use your old street address, 'cause it will take a while for things to catch up with your homelessness. Some store looking for warehouse help ain't gonna mail you nothing right away, and if you get a job you can always change it later. Same for listing a phone number, as this was all before they had cheap pay-as-you-go cell phones, a real gift to the working poor, showing how everything adapts to new markets. Put down your old house telephone number, 'cause the phone company usually don't reassign it for a year to two. Nobody can call you with work of course, so just walk back in a few days and say you thought you got a message from them but it was garbled. That makes you seem eager even.

By the way, don't try and look for work on-line early Monday mornings, when it's all just slush left over from Friday. For getting jobs, shaving in the car is hard, but I learned from another guy to use sex lube instead of shaving cream. Smells kinda nice. The not-oil kind—it wipes right off with no water, and is smooth enough to work with a dull razor.

Oh, and if you got good clothes you're saving for a good job, give them to the dry cleaners and just don't pick them up until you're ready. The dry cleaners are your closet. Most say ninety days and out, but why would they throw away a customer's shit? They ain't gonna get rich doing business that way. And good shoes are life. You're outside a lot in the weather, and move around a lot more than you're used to. Get used to sleeping in your shoes too, so they don't get stolen and so you can run away quick if you need to. If homelessness had a dress code, it'd include tore-up shoes. Try and keep 'em clean.

After a while the coffee shop people start to know you, and the customers start to shy away instead of lending you their phone on the excuse that you forgot yours. They all know by the way you look that you have no job, and that makes you not one of them, so courtesy stops applying. New rules. You start waiting around parking lots for day work, competing with the immigrants for whatever someone will offer until even that starts to fail, the boss looking at you and knowing he can't bring you into a customer's house even to paint.

Stealing food is where the bus stops next. In fact, it's how I first met Casey. Nobody is proud of stealing, but nobody is proud of being hungry either, and it often ends up you choosing between one or the other. Hunger always wins—it's biology. Those songs about freedom being nothing left to lose, and the purity of life without the burden of possessions are bullshit. Nobody who woke up hungry after going to bed hungry without knowing when they'll eat next sings.

I never stole money, and I never stole from people. I only stole things from things. If a thing could own a business, then I could steal from a thing. So I'd stand up at the fast-food place like I was gonna order, then grab something off the counter and run. Dining and dashing, hoping it wasn't a fish sandwich, which I don't care for, but beggars can't be choosers, right? Important to keep your sense of humor if you can, too. I looked back a few times, but none of the workers was ever gonna chase me, what the hell did they care—they just made up another kids meal for what I stole, and they did it fast. Too slow satisfying the customer and they'd lose their jobs and join my jamboree. Workers like them know they can be fired for anything or nothing, so what do they care about me? When the company tells you it's minimum wage 'cause they can't by law get away with paying you less, it kinda gets into your head, and you start to believe what they say.

I tried to do this kind of stealing as little as I could, but the dirtier you get and the more you sleep out, the less chance anyone is going to give you work. Some fast food places will let you sit and warm up, and some see you homeless and treat you like you got the plague. Try 'em, one by one, you got the time, or ask around.

I grabbed a good–sized bag off the fast food counter that one day and headed to the door, only to run whack into this guy coming in. First time I ever saw him. The counter trash must've had a bad day or something, because she screamed I was a thief and I felt no strength to push past, or fight. If a place with so much food being thrown away wouldn't spot me a Happy Time

Meal Box, fuck 'em, I'd go to jail and eat there. Society cares a lot more it seems about feeding a criminal than a hungry man.

"Imagine that," the guy said to me, "A man willing to go to jail for seven dollars. I'll pay for it."

"Thanks."

"It's okay, I've had hard times too. Want to sit down? What's your name?"

"Uh, Gilligan."

"No it's not. What's your name?"

"Spiderman."

"C'mon brother, sit down. I'll buy coffee."

"Thanks buddy, but I ain't like that. You go somewhere else for that."

Hell, a lot of guys did a lot of bad things for money, only thing they had left to sell I guess, and he wouldn't have been the first to try with me. I had no job, and they wanted me to have no soul.

"No, no, I'm a preacher. I'm Casey, call me Preacher Casey if you like. I run a shelter at Calvary Church. You're welcome here for coffee, and you're welcome there. You can take the bus, Number 3A. If the driver is Robby, with the dreads, tell him Casey'll pay later. Drop you right at Calvary. He knows."

So people laugh at you because you were once the shoemaker and now you walk around barefoot. Well, buddy, things can change pretty fast. Back in Reeve a million years ago I had gone to the factory with my father looking for work, but they said they no longer hired "entry levels" or "apprentices." They wanted younger men who would work for less, but who already knew more or less what the older men who worked for more did. The new owners cut back to one shift, then sub-divided the jobs so that one man did not need to know very much. That made 'em easier to hire but mostly easier to fire and replace, modular-like. The deal was, take my dad's friends' jobs for less money. My friends would take my dad's job. That would last for a while, until the whole plant closed down and the land was sold to developers. Might be jobs in the retail store they planned to build, I was told while security walked us the way out. At least the economy created some new jobs for those guys. That was it for me and the factory, top of the heap, best job I never had.

I tried to get by for a while on public assistance, to eat. Food stamps sounds like something from an old movie; the first version of the program was created during the Depression, so I guess it fits. Now it's called Supplemental Nutrition Assistance Program, or, to make you feel stupid while feeling ashamed, SNAP. In Ohio they pay us out the whole state on the first of the month, millions of people—Pay Day, Food Day, Mother's Day. Most stores open early and stay open late that day, 'cause most people don't—or can't—budget well, and they're pretty hungry come the Day, kind of a mini-economic boom. It's the government keeping families—and businesses—sort of alive, thirty days at a time. The use of actual stamps for food has been replaced by EBT and debit cards, so you can't sell off some of the stamps for liquor money. I qualified for all of $200 a month, and that's being cut across the board to save on tax money for the government to spend on more important stuff. I'm pretty skinny, but only $50 a week for food is hard, my friend, hard. I'm just one guy, and I can skip a meal if I need to, and I do. But it seems like in Reeve these days, a lot of families with kids don't have enough to eat, and a lot of them are getting some SNAP money to get by. To me, that is a crime, same as burning down their houses.

After you solve the eating problem, you gotta tend to the sleeping problem. I'd held on to my old car as long as I could. But you quickly learn that you can't just park a car anywhere and live in it. Stay away from schools, cops are always watching out for perverts. Churches are better, except on Sundays when people come to pray and need the parking spaces to get closer to God. Best thing to do is hide your clothes in the trunk so no one steals them, and it's less obvious you're living there. During the cold months, get a car cover, one of those canvas things, and nobody knows you're sleeping all cozy inside. That isn't much help in the hot times when the mosquitoes chew you apart 'cause you gotta leave the windows down. Keep in mind while a car parked at night attracts all sorts of attention, one parked in a shopping center in the daytime is just fine. "Just taking a nap, officer, while the little woman shops for God-knows-what. Heh heh, you know how it is. You too, have a good day, officer." If they think you're just resting between buying things, you're still on the right track and okay. The poor world is a dark place in some ways, but finding a dark enough place to sleep makes you like a shark, always swimming.

At night, when the stores close, you become the enemy. You obviously ain't there to buy things, so you are not wanted or welcomed. Even if the place is open late, cops have been patrolling twenty-four hour stores' lots longer than you've been homeless and know who is consuming and who is trying to sleep. Wal-Mart makes a big deal of offering overnight space to

RVs as a sales gimmick, because those people buy shit, but unless your car is an RV or you buy shit, you are unwelcome. Wal-Mart don't want us 'cause there is nothing left for them to take from us.

Still not sure how it works, brother? The cops will watch over you like guardian angels when you camp out on the sidewalk in front of the Apple store before they're ready to sell something new and you got money.

Location, location, location.

Modern architecture now accounts for us homeless, putting metal bars on ledges and benches so it's impossible to lay down. Stuff like that's invisible to most people, but for us it marks a spot like dog scent: this is mine, not yours, go away. Nobody wants a homeless person around, and I guess I can't blame them. Takes some getting used to, though. At first when someone wanted me to move on, I'd think "It's a public park bench. Why can't I sit on it all day if I want to? There a law?" and I'd get angry, bark back. But sooner than later I'd just move on, same as the wind would blow newspapers off the same bench. Days I'd feel like a ghost wearing a Halloween Earl mask. If you got money you can tell homeless people where they can sit. Most times though there wasn't any law about how long you could sit on a bench, just a sense that we wasn't supposed to be there. Laws nobody made are the easiest to break.

So overall, friends, sleeping outside is tough. Cough syrup works if you're gonna try without getting too drunk every night. After a while you'll probably be ill anyway, so it ain't really cheating. You're always worried about getting sick, but in the end the most contagious thing you encounter is despair. Most cops'll just move you along if you don't give them guff, but watch out for the odd one with an attitude. The ones to really watch out for, though, are private security, rent-a-cops. Those guys got no oversight and usually want to impress whoever is paying them, and they'll kick your ass for the fun of it. It's a new economy business—a good portion of our labor force is focused on protection rather than production.

So that's eating and sleeping. Next is the toilet stuff. Gas stations are filthy, but you can usually get in. Fast-food toilets are cleaner but sometimes the manager won't let you in without buying something, and they're always watching. Best is the ones in a supermarket, except they are always in the back and you have to make it through the store. And don't fucking steal the toilet paper for later, because I might be the next one in.

It takes three things to get clean, hot water, soap and towels, but hitting the trifecta is rare. You don't get to bathe much, and washing up in a sink only goes so far. Baby wipes are pretty good if you don't have running water. The first time in two weeks you actually are someplace you can take off all your clothes it'll feel weird to be naked again. I do remember the first time I had to go for a while without a shower. I didn't feel right. I smelled a bit, more like old clothes though 'cause I wasn't so much dirty like with real dirt as I just smelled too much like, well, me, I guess. Maybe if I lived in Africa or somewhere poor it'd be okay, but here it was un-American. My hair itched, and other places too. I kept wiping my hands and face with McDonald's napkins, trying to wash up in public restrooms without soap, but being unwashed kinda became how I was, like having a cold, a new state. When I had begged up enough for a night in a motel, it was like every part of me felt better as that warm water poured over my body. I turned it up hotter than Hell, because I could. I made some lather, and felt my hands over my own body in ways and places like I used to do. Sometimes I'd go deep-dish, soaking up to my nose in the tub. I tried to rub the soap into my skin so I could smell like I had a job again.

It gets real shitty out there when no one cares what happens to you. No matter what you don't have, someone else has less and wants yours. I nearly lost an eye over a pair of boots, got razor-cut because of a jacket. The best way to win a fight is not to be in a fight, so stay away from other people, sheep attract wolves. That band of brothers shit works in hobo movies and folk songs, but not in America where we are too good at business to allow opportunities to pass by. Yes, the romanticized fantasy of street living is entertaining right up until the first time you get your jaw busted over a pair of warm gloves, a soiled old bed quilt, or two dollars' worth of dimes.

You may want a knife or even a gun, but don't get caught with either by the cops, because your best defense to the police is appearing innocent, poor and smelly, but at the same time boring and safe. Lockup sounds like free food and a clean bed, until you been there. Jail is full of criminals, and if your crime is just being homeless, everyone else is going to be meaner and tougher. The people who run the jail could care less what happens inside, and it's easy to get fucked up over who gets to use the one toilet first, or who gets the last serving of lunch. Stay there more than a night or two, and you start looking for someone even weaker than yourself to push around. I did it, pushed some twink aside to grab his breakfast, but it isn't like normal stealing—it feels worse.

I can tell you that the risks include being physically and sexually assaulted on a regular and ongoing basis, in or out of jail. This is an eventuality, not just a possibility, especially if you are a woman, or a thin-slight young man, because without things to affirm you as a member of society, you are just prey. Sometimes it feels like worse just gets worse.

ON THE BUS, Casey remembered to me that first time the two of us met and was starting to get to know each other at that fast food place.

"So, Earl, is it? What brought you to homelessness?"

"I ain't really homeless, Preacher Casey. I just can't find work."

"Drugs? Alcohol? Been arrested for anything serious? Done any real time?"

"I just can't find work."

"You taking your meds? You not taking your meds? Got to talk out some problems? Can't get along with people? Vet?"

"I grew up in a working family, Preacher. My grandpa and my dad both worked in the same factory here in Reeve. Now it's gone, being developed."

"Developed? What's that mean?"

"Means I ain't got a job, and if I get one it'll be part-time in a store."

"Owe child support? Busted parole? Killed a man? Abused? Abusive?"

"I ain't committed no crime, but some food stealing, like you saw."

"Come on man, you sound like you got most of a high school education, you look like you can stand a day's work. You aren't stupid. What's your dope?"

"The jobs I was planning on disappeared. The jobs my dad did went to Japan, then to China, then Vietnam, then someplace even cheaper they found. The stuff I learned in high school turned out not to be skills anymore. I took Home Ec with my girlfriend, so I went for work at a bakery in Gibbsville, but they wanted programmers, not bakers, and said most employees don't have a clue how to bake bread. I thought working hard would help, but every job I got was broken down into little steps so it was easy, so easy that hard work didn't matter. Even when I tried to impress the boss, you know, do a little extra, stay a little later, he just cleared me out when profits fell that quarter, saying it was overhead—fuck, I was overhead. He'd hire someone back someday if he needed the help, but for now, corporate headquarters was on his ass demanding cost savings. Said nothing personal, he was just doing his job by getting rid of mine. I went back a month later to see him and beg, but he'd been downsized himself, so keep an extra bed open."

"Well, you can stay at our shelter for a while, get back on your feet."

"My feet is fine, preacher. My hands is fine. My head is fine. I don't need a place to shelter—what am I hiding from? I need a place to work, is all."

"Either way man, c'mon in."

I had been to some shelters before. A lot were just for women, and their young kids, as often times older boys of say fourteen years old were sent to the adult men's shelters where sadly some of my brothers fed on them.

I was in pretty bad shape, but it was nothing compared to a woman trying to find work, living in a shelter, trying to feed her kids alongside herself. I thought of Jodie from Bullseye, but at least she had that job. Where can you leave the kids that's safe during the day when you're out looking for a job—shelter don't wanna babysit them. Even the clean shelters smelled dirty, in the way a hospital does. For me, most of the places that weren't always full, or full of people so far outta their minds that they were dangerous, were part of some religious thing, but not like Preacher Casey's turned out to be. The other places start off acting like they want to help you, but they end up selling you something, same as if you're at the store. Price of a meal is listening to some God talk, same as the price of watching Monday Night Football is seeing commercials for trucks and credit cards. If you don't say "Praise God" often enough and sound like you're havin' a squirt for 'em, they throw you out. What do I want from God, Father? Same as I want from anyone—give me a job to do.

Now, this is not to disrespect. Religion was important in Reeve, and some said we had more pews than people. We all believed in God, the Baby Jesus and the Holy Spirit, but in leavened amounts. Preacher had sixty minutes on Sundays to make his point and Amen, maybe ninety minutes around the holidays. People kept their religion to themselves, and anyone walking around town knocking on doors with some new Word was more likely to be met with an angry dog than a sympathetic ear. We understood that getting along meant you could only be so selfish, that only watching out for yourself just would not work in a place where we had to live together. Sermon on the Mount said all that Casey told me, but we did it on our own in a practical way. I guess you can make a life outta not getting along if you only read one book, hating on certain people because one page of the Bible says to, while ignoring the rest of what it says, which is pretty goddamn clear about love.

Casey was still laughing on the bus when I remembered telling him that. Casey said:

"God focuses on the big issues, who we are, what we make of ourselves, maybe most of all how we treat others. As for myself, I'm a preacher. I play for the team of angels, but I'm not always one of them. But imperfect is just a step. You come on by the shelter, keep your nose clean, help out a little, and God and me'll not worry too much about the rest."

Casey and me ended up talking a lot as we became friends. Casey read a lot of books. He seemed to understand things that had happened around me and my life in a way that made it clear that Reeve was not an island like we thought it was. In fact, what had happened to us here had happened to a lot of places. A "hollowing out," Casey said, in a kind of sermon of his own:

"Earl, money isn't spread around like it used to be. After the war, until about the time you were in junior high school, incomes rose at the same level for everyone. But then things changed—you saw it, your mom and dad for sure. The top one percent of Americans watched their income grow dozens of times more than the rest of us, until that same small group of people held forty percent of all the wealth in the U.S."

"Look at Detroit," Casey went on, "my old hometown. The U.S. emerged from the Second World War with Heaven's only functioning army, with more than half of the industrial capacity in the world and as banker and creditor to allies and enemies. That was the highest hill our country climbed, and Detroit sat at the summit. Detroit was looking into a future where the rising prosperity was going to fuel a demand for cars unlike any consumer demand in human history. There was so much money and growth and potential that everyone ate well. When it rains like that, people can't help but get wet. My own father started as a toolmaker's apprentice right after high school and ended up making $35 an hour, with a pension, health care, employee discounts on the cars he helped build and a union picnic every Fourth of July."

"Detroit rode that all up until about 1973, when everything went over the hill, not just in Detroit, but most everywhere— wages fell, benefits fell, production fell, population fell, home values fell. You can buy a house in Detroit for $6,000 today. Greatest generation and all, no, they were the greatest exception. It all happened quickly, in only the course of a few decades, two or three generations. My dad got out okay, but my older brother didn't. He told me he felt thrown away, that he never thought this was so fragile. I hate to say it so crudely—God forgive me— but America lost its balls."

"C'mon Casey," I said, "that's what business does, even I know that. It's their job to make as much money as they can for them, not for us. A dog can't help being a dog, so you don't kick at him for peeing on a tree, right?"

"Earl, I'm not talking about anything radical here. I'm talking about a little bit of a balance. Those fights between your mom and dad over money you told me about, they were real. They were talking to each other about what was happening in America, all around them, without even knowing it. A very few people were choosing for them. Business became all appetite. Now we are reaching for a zero-sum point where wealthy people believe that to gain anything requires them to take it from someone else. Wal-Mart already makes billions, but it fights even tiny increases to the minimum wage. If McDonald's doubled its employees' salaries to $14.50 an hour, a Big Mac would cost only 68 cents more. Actually, even all this talk about minimum wage is missing a big point: more Americans work for sub-minimum than for minimum wage. People who might get tips only have to be paid $2.13 an hour in some places. And that $2.13 has not changed by law in twenty-two years due to lobbying by the restaurant business. Owners are doing okay, as restaurant prices have gone up in the last twenty-two years. Just like in Roman times, the lion's share beats the Christians' share any day."

"This is where my religious and political views meet up, Earl, kinda like how you and me met up. Most wealthy folks say they're religious people, but when the churches are rich and the regular people poor, you gotta wonder who is serving who. Most of those wealthy ignore one of the highest ideals from the Sermon—caring. Those words aren't just some more poetry of hopefulness that passes for Christianity. He said quite clearly, 'they who hunger and thirst for righteousness, they should be satisfied.' But it ain't just about handing over a few crumbs, saying it's better than no bread at all. Getting into Heaven isn't about earning merit badges, here's one for those canned goods you didn't want anyway at Christmas or another for tossing change into a cup. It's about how you live a life in total, what you do 99 percent of the time, what you make of the world you live in. It isn't religion that's wrong, same as it isn't business that's wrong. It's greed and selfishness that's wrong, no matter what channel you're watching."

I always thought the Bible was like the dictionary, all the words was inside and you could scramble them around to mean anything you like, but Casey made sense.

"Look Earl, even though the original Owner was barefooted, what happens upstairs in my church is that as soon as some expensive shoes hit that floor it seems like the place loses its purpose. Me, I preached for the Lord a long time, but some days I think God's the laziest man on earth. What I want is to be able to look out over my congregation and say to them forget most of what I've said but go out and be kind to each other, help each other and walk humbly when you have something others still need. When they hear someone cry in America because they're hungry, I want that to be louder in their ears than any sermon."

"So okay, Preacher, when's it going to get better? When are we going to be able to live like our grandparents did?"

"Earl, nostalgia isn't history. This is a story about change, and it's important for you to know how that happened. Here we are forty years on still talking about recovery like it was as real as an election year promise. Prosperity is not something that will follow if we simply wait long enough. Like my friend says, cut through all the lies and there it is, right in front of you: America used to be a developing nation, in the best sense of that word. Almost in spite of themselves, the robber barons built prosperity through jobs. We had to get past the horrors of enslaving other human beings, past making children work in factories, past killing men in mines and machines. There were dark times, criminal times, but people had a sense of 'we'll get past this.' Then we crossed a line. Manufacturing in America became expensive. Businesses sought lower costs and higher profits. String that out as far as it goes and it means paying workers as close to zero—or zero if you somehow could like with slavery—and pulling in as much profit—as close to one hundred percent—as you somehow could. The question seemed to have become, 'How many miles can you drive on a gallon of our blood?' We watched a reversal of two hundred years. American workers never earned as much again as they did in 1973. It was soon after that someone laid off a steelworker who became Patient Zero of the new economy."

"The numbers are too consistent, the lines too straight. This was no accident, no invisible hand. Earl, we changed from a place that made things—radiators, cash registers, gaskets, ball bearings, TVs—into a place that just makes deals. Making things creates jobs, and jobs create prosperity. Making deals just creates wealth for the dealers. It's math. The money that went up had to come from somewhere. That was Reeve, right out of your father's pocket. The deal makers don't care because they don't live here, hell, they don't live anywhere. We live here."

✍   ✍   ✍

It was somewhere in there that my old man finally fell apart like a cardboard box in the rain. He died just like I expected, word coming in the form of a late night phone call from Mom. I put the phone down, sitting up in bed, wishing maybe I smoked so I had something to do with my hands, and remembered a last visit, him in the old folks home or the hospital, I don't recall which. His skin was wrinkling like how bacon looks frying, but so thin you could see the veins blue under there. The doctors said it was the stroke, maybe caused by the liquor, but to me what killed him was the tension of being him, holding whatever it was inside him, never letting the poison out. When I was young that thing in there was a mystery, maybe something cool I thought, like he was a war hero, maybe even a spy and couldn't talk about it. Over the years I began to think it wasn't that he couldn't talk about it, as much as he just wouldn't. At the hospital or wherever it was that last time, I remember him trying to take his pills. They came in little paper cups, and I watched him dump them onto his tray. His hands shook, and his fingers were so dry and fragile, he couldn't get them pills up to his mouth. I was sittin' right there, but he wouldn't say a word to me, just tried to wet his fingertips from the corner of his mouth, so the pill would stick to his finger and he could get it onto his tongue. He tried and tried, finally reaching over for the call button to the Puerto Rican attendant who came and silently pushed the pill into his mouth while I sat there. I imagined her when he died, looking at her cheap watch and thinking about whatever paperwork they had to do when another one passed.

As a kid, I never understood funerals. The person was dead and no amount of pound cake, covered casseroles and flowers

176

was gonna fix that. I got over-dressed up against my will and dragged out to my grandpa's and then my grandma's funerals to sit and watch people cry while I struggled to unbutton my shirt collar. Funerals were big affairs in Reeve, because growing up, living and dying in the same town left a lot of loose ends to tie up. I came to understand that these funerals were for the living, to figure out what to do with the memories, decide which connections were gonna stay intact and which were gonna, well, die. My grandparents passed when I was still a kid, old enough to be sad, but mostly just 'cause I knew I wasn't gonna see them again, like death just made things permanently inconvenient. With my old man, the memories were funny colors I didn't fully understand yet, mostly too fresh to have been washed and folded away neatly the way time does.

We had the wake for him at the VFW hall. It would have been wrong to make much out of the church part, but he was a drinker and so it seemed appropriate to gather at a bar. It was a pale Wednesday morning outside, but inside it was dark and damp and whatever day you wanted it to be, and eternally felt like 3 a.m. I recognized a lot of the people, odd though, them seeing me mostly for the first time as an adult. I got tired of decrepit men and pinched old women coming up to me and saying, "It's Ray's boy, Earl," like me and him were always tied together that way. My mom wasn't talking much, and I found shelter at the end of the bar. The door to the kitchen kept swinging open, the sticky green fluorescent flash half interrupting me and half keeping me awake as I looked to set down the burden I carried around from my old man.

"You know Ray?" said the guy who was riding the bar stool hard right to me. Stubbed out a butt, lit another one. Teeth stained yellow from a lifetime of unfiltered Camels. Thin lips, just a line.

"Smoke?" he said to me.

"Nah, thanks."

"I hear you. I've been trying to quit for thirty years. Sure you don't want one?"

"Thanks, no mister. So how'd you know Ray?"

"Me and Ray served together in Korea. I hadn't talked to him but maybe twice since, then two days ago Sissy found my name in some of Ray's old stuff and called me. I drove down here to say goodbye."

"Not from Reeve then?"

"Nah, home is near Pittsburgh."

"Steel?"

"Yep. Thirty years on the big bucket, pouring out two hundred tons of steel a day. Lookit my right arm—muscle's twice as thick as on the left 'cause of that lever I pulled every day. I got that job right after Korea in fact. My old man sent me to see the foreman while I was still wearing my uniform."

"How's it up there now? I heard the president say he's creating more jobs, so I was considering moving up."

"Moving on isn't a bad idea. I wished I had done it at your age. Hell, I wished I'd done it last month."

"So there's work where you're from?"

"Same there as it was four years ago and four years before that. Every four years the president comes back into western Pennsylvania like a dog looking for a place to pee. He reminds us that his wife's cousin is from some town near to ours, gets photographed at the diner if it's still in business, and then makes those promises to us while winking at the big business donors who feed him bribes they call campaign contributions. I'm tempted to cut out the middle man and just write in 'Goldman Sachs' on my ballot next election.

Another cigarette.

"Smoke?"

"Nah."

"Meanwhile the coast reporters will write another story about the 'heartland' and then get out as fast as they can, acting as if something might stick to them if they stood still too long. We got so few families in town anymore we can't hardly come up with a football team. I had to drive thirty miles last week to find a dentist, nobody closer still in business. The new mayor has this idea of encouraging art galleries and boutiques to take up in vacant buildings to revive the economy. So that's us now, building a country on boutiques."

He cupped his smoke in his hand, hiding the orange dot at the end just like those soldiers in the war movies on TV did, like there was gonna be a Nazi sniper there in the VFW hall or something.

"Helps me remember," he said. "Remembering's the only thing I got."

Some kid slipped up to the bar.

"Were you were a soldier, sir? Thank you for your service. You're a hero, sir."

The drunk barely looked up. Made it seem like his head was too heavy to lift.

179

"Was in Korea. I wasn't no hero. Don't thank me for what I did, 'cause you don't have any idea. No fucking idea."

"Sorry sir, see, I'm going to enlist, and I wanted to thank you for protecting us."

"Get away now son, there's dangerous objects around here."

The kid popped away, more confused and threatened than chastised.

Back to me and the drunk.

"So, I guess Ray and you had a pretty good time over there in Korea. To hear him tell it, it was all booze and broads."

"Is that what he said? My memory is a little soggy right now, more like a scar to me even when it's working right, but I seem to recall it a little different." It was a smile, but shaped like a sickle the farmers around Reeve used to use. "Name's Miles by the way."

"Hey Miles, I'm Earl. Lemme buy the next round. I'm drinking beer. You?"

"Whiskey. Beer's a good foundation, but it don't have the octane no more, just leaves me drowsy."

I should've known. He had empty shot glasses lined up on the bar like they were on sale on a shelf at Bullseye.

"So c'mon Miles, how was Korea, really?"

"There wasn't a whole lot of broads anywhere near us and damn little booze. Mostly local-made hooch that kids would wander up and trade us for C-rat cans of Spam and some goop called 'Fruit, Peach, Canned, Syrup-Type.' The Korean kids would wear tin cans salvaged from us around their necks, clanging and clinking to warn us they were comin'. I learned how to say 'hello' in their language, so I'd yell that at them. But it wasn't no fun. Ray and me spent most of our war on some fucked-up hill freezing our asses off."

"Is that so Miles?" I said. "So old Ray was a liar then in addition to everything else. To hear him talk about Korea and the service, you'd think it was New Year's Eve with a cherry on top every night."

"Isn't my place to talk ill of the dead, but Korea was no cherry. Look at me—throw a white ball against a dirty wall and it comes back dirty every time. I never had no great dream, and in return I never expected to feel like this. I came back a drunk and have been happy to be one every damn day since. Thinking on what made me start drinking is worse than all this any time, my young friend. Hand me them cigarettes, willya? You want one? Cheers."

He threw back a shot, then another one right on top of it. In the light of the kitchen door swinging open, I could now see he was a real old-school rummy, a catalog of tells. Light bulb nose, red spiderwebbed veins in his eyes, broken blood vessels on his face, tobacco-stained voice, lots of old blue bruises from falling down, skin yellowed from the jaundice, like Grandma would say about Grandpa. It took years of whiskey for that. You get there different ways, but in the end pain is all the same. The trip's all you have until you arrive, right? You had to have a reason to keep working at it that long, 'cause the fun of drinking must've passed away a long while ago.

"So c'mon, what was it really like, Miles?"

"Korea? Ray? You keep asking me—you really wanna know? I'll tell you: we threw snowballs at each other, so okay, there, now you know, smart guy. You think we hadda choice out there?

Fuck no, just like here, now, we did what we was told and then shit we couldn't control happened to us. What more you want from me boy, to confess to my sins? You think you're some sorta preacher? You think I don't have a reason, hell, a right, to stay quiet and just drink myself to death?"

Another old timer came up, spilling beer on me as he tried to regain his balance, then bumping into me as he had to choose between that and spilling even more beer. I wrinkled my nose at the smell of too much cologne. Lotta these yahoos around here don't know about dressing up. Tie never tied right, you can spot them a mile away.

"Oh Earl, that you? Goddamn, honey look, it's Ray's boy, all grown up. I ain't seen you for years. Sorry about your old man. You wanna 'nother drink son?"

"You're Ray's son?" said Miles. "He had a son? He never told me."

"Yeah, that's me, um, what was it, Miles? And he never told me about you neither, so go kiss my ass."

"Well, if Ray didn't find the reason to tell you any stories about Korea, then it isn't my job. I ain't your father, thank God for that. You seen it all every day anyway, him drinking, it was written on his fucking face same as me. Now c'mon, we're enjoying a friendly drink here in Ray's name. Let's just have a toast to the old son of a bitch and leave it there. He's dead now, got his new job to do, so let's cover him up and let him get to it. To the dead, may they stay buried! You wanna smoke? Here, pass me the pack."

❧   ❧   ❧

ONE NIGHT AFTER dinner at the shelter we all got to talking.

"Preacher, we heard in Reeve that it was the immigrants, Koreans I guess, who took all the jobs at lower wages. Ain't that what's always been said?"

"Yeah, preacher, what about America for Americans?"

"Everyone of us are the sons of immigrants," Casey said, "so don't be foolish about Koreans."

"But we was here first, preacher."

"Unless your name is Chief Full-of-Shit, shut the hell up and listen to the preacher now."

"It used to be the Irish who took all the jobs, then it was, who? Maybe the Italians next? I forget," said Casey. "I can't keep hate in chronological order any more. I think the Mexicans were blamed after that. See many Koreans in your factory in Reeve before it closed? No, of course not. Immigrants will lower the low-end wages certainly. Plenty of them too, so they are easy to hire and fire, disposable labor, spare parts. But you've seen the Koreans in Reeve and none of their small business places took any jobs from you, and may even have created a few. We don't need fewer workers, we need more decent jobs."

"But I've seen on TV they said the economy added thousands of jobs this month, so that's good, right?"

"Yeah maybe, but those are likely mostly minimum wage jobs. Like eating all your daily calories as candy—"

"—Or booze if you're Earl."

"Shut up. Preacher, you know I'll take any job. I just want to work. I still know how to sweat."

"Easy, Earl, I believe you. But even if you'll accept a lower wage, how far is a couple of dollars an hour throwing construction crap into a Dumpster going to get you? What if they did pay you minimum wage. How far is seven bucks an hour going to go? We're back to thinking a few crumbs is better than no bread at all. You going to do five hours of labor for the phone bill? Another ten for the groceries each week? Another twenty or thirty for a car payment? How many hours you going to work? How many can you work? Nobody can make a living doing those jobs, even if you have two or three of them. You can't raise a family on minimum wage. And you can't build a nation on the working poor. Pull yourself up by your bootstraps, folks say, as a way of blaming the working poor for being swept up in a change they don't have a snowball's chance in hell against."

"But the jobs will come back someday . . . right?"

"No," Casey said, in that way he had of being patient and frustrated at the same time, "the system is reaching for its natural conclusion. The lines of lower costs and higher profits are converging. My friend says, 'A rising tide lifts all yachts.' Our society is dividing into a very narrow band of the super wealthy, and us—everyone else—what they call the working poor. This has been a mass migration, an Apartheid of dollars, money leaving the majority of us into the hands of just a few. Saying today it is one versus 99 is probably wrong in the absolute percentages but dead solid perfect as an indicator. Reeve isn't the exception. You just got hit in the back of the head earlier than most."

"What concerns me deeper is the effect this is having on people not working—or working at deskilled jobs. For things to be better, you have to be able to wake yourself up, swap yesterday for a another shot at tomorrow, and too many of us stopped being capable of that. We broke down. Like bending metal, you can never get it back to its original state. You lose your resistance to sorrow. Work earns you money, but a job creates some value in yourself. Jesus said on the Mount, 'You are the salt of the earth. But if the salt loses its savor, how can it be made salty again? It is no longer good for anything.' Some chance to feel you contributed, made something, did something, accomplished something, however small and likely unimportant, that's inside us. I'm a preacher and so I'll call it a soul. That was taken away. Without a soul, that salt, there is no hope, no redemption. You don't just scroll to the bottom and click accept. Work saved more souls than most preachers."

MEN WOULD COME and go from the shelter. Most were passing through the area, looking for work or too crazy to know where they were, but feeling better because they were moving. Casey would take them all in. When we talked all together, usually only when Casey was there to kinda supervise things, it was like we were those Christmas ghosts, asking each other who we used to be when we were still alive.

"So what'd you do before you ended up homeless?" asked Casey of one.

"Used to be a machinist at the Stolle aluminum stamping plant."

"Never heard of it. Not from around here then? Where you from?"

"Well, most recently I guess, from McAlester."

"Long trip?"

"You could say that, Preacher. Took me four years, minus 28 days good behavior to get here."

"I understand, brother. If you don't mind me askin' . . ."

"I'm used to it, no mind, especially from a preacher. After I lost my job I got caught selling weed. That's all that people in my town was ready to buy. Family had to eat is why."

"And your family?"

"Aw, Preacher, I guess it was God's will that they had to leave me. While I was inside, the bank closed our account, sayin' they had a policy of not conducting business with felons, or I guess, felons' wives. Insurance company, too. Both were big companies you know, name brands even."

"I'm sorry man."

"It's okay. My wife got her old name back in the divorce so she was marked to do business again. She said when I get back on my feet I can probably see the kids, so it'll be alright, with the God's help I'm hoping to become worthy enough to receive."

"What about you, brother?" asked Casey.

"Me, came back from overseas. I tried to kill myself in the garage. I almost did to myself what the terrorists couldn't, but my fiancée talked me into takin' the gun outta my mouth. I never forgave her. So I left."

"What happened to that hand?"

"I left it on a street in Basra. IED. Fucking squid corpsman saved my life, stopped the bleeding right there in the dust, screaming like some nut case, 'Fuck you God, you ain't gonna get this one, this is my Marine.' The Corps gave me this robohand, works pretty good for most things, but then again, I can't feel my daughter's hair with it—"

"And you can't jack off with it neither, so stop feeling sorry for yourself."

"Fuck off man, I do okay. Thing is, when I go for a job people either stare at me, or they freaking won't look at me."

"Yo, I was in Iraq too, Preacher, but my job was to build shit for those people, schools and houses, so they'd like us. Freakin' hearts and minds, same as in Vietnam movies. But now I'm home and seeing my home town looking like Fallujah. I wanna ask every fucking politician for everything we built in the sandbox, build two here at home. For every one of us soldiers, hire the same number of people here to work, at the same pay and the same benefits. When the politician says we can't pay for that, I wanna tell 'em to pay for it exactly the same way they paid for it when it was happening overseas. When they say we had to spend the money over there to defend America, I'll say that a job for me in America defends America better than any killing does—unless we just fucking start putting rounds into the unemployed."

"Ask the bastards," said Casey, "where they got the four trillion dollars for the bailouts of 2008 and 2009, and how many new jobs that didn't create, and why banks that spent more money on lobbying got more bailout money. And about how that home mortgage thing represented years of middle class gains sucked upward, a massive redistribution of wealth."

"Amen to that."

"Me, over here, Preacher. I was one of those mortgages. See, I was a computer programmer. I made good money, riding the boom up. I had a nice house, too, one of those new big ones, with a soaking tub and rain shower. Then my salary was cut, then my hours, then I was told to work from home, then my job moved to Bangalore. Bank took the house. It isn't fair. I always voted for the candidate that promised lower taxes for business to create jobs. I did what I was supposed to do, right? Now I see all that stuff on Fox about how great it is here and think I woke up in the wrong country."

"Okay, there it is. Now you white people are starting to feel our pain. Good for you suckers."

"Yeah, you wait brother, in a year or two this pain will all be suburbanized. Your turn is comin' rich boys."

"Hell yes. Look around. Once upon a time them check cashing places and payday loans, they was only in the inner city, fucking slums and ghettos, man. Now they're out here. How'd that happen?"

"You are all pathetic man. Look at you. All you white dudes. I'm unemployed and homeless and freaking black, so stop your bitching. You all gonna have jobs someday, and I'll still be here living in this preacher's damn basement."

"You right man. That's how it always was, how it is, and how it's gonna be. We are still on the plantation as far as most are concerned. You tell them dumb white fucks."

"You all—we all—are niggers."

"You watch that shit—you callin' us white guys niggers now?"

"Now? We've all been America's niggers for a long time. Some of us black guys just knew it sooner."

The room was hot. We weren't supposed to talk about race. We didn't know how to, anyways. Casey stood up. He had that look, the one where he knows what he's gonna say even if you don't have a clue what's the right thing to do. He'd been here before.

"What you say has a lot of truth," Casey began.

"Blacks are unemployed almost twice the rate of whites. Black men go to prison at higher rates, die of gunshot wounds at higher rates. It's a sad legacy. But you are holding the shittier tip of the same shitty stick. Before we all got told we were white, a lot of people in this town hated the Polacks, or the Hunkies, the Jews or the Wops. It did us no good. Way back, the bosses used the new Irish immigrants to break strikes, keeping them separate from the rest of the town and playing off Catholic-Protestant prejudices the immigrants had packed in their trunks alongside their Bibles. It's an old trick. Works nearly every time, too."

"Look, until we understand at a gut level we are all in this together, if we keep thinking black and white and never see the whole 99 percent of us are dirty gray, we'll never get anywhere. We need to think leveling up, not leveling down to create an economy, hell, a society, that is sustainable. That's the word—sustainable—because what we are doing now is gonna kill us all."

THERE WAS ONE guy, younger than me, spent a few weeks at the shelter. He helped out, but didn't say much. In that kind of place, you don't ask because you don't know what a man is carrying with him. Some might have guns or knives, some might be carrying something far more deadly inside their head. A lot of them were just angry, and angry often turned to mean. There was a whole industry out there now that fed them and fed off them, hours of talk radio picking up and then handing back to them their anger turned to cynicism, of course with commercials.

Casey remembered to me on the bus:

"I was probably the only one who knew his name, and only because I asked him when we first met and he was being polite, hoping for a space at the shelter. I never had any reason to use his name, however. Never needed to call him. We'd eat and he'd clean on his own, he'd be up and outside raking leaves or shoveling snow without me asking, disappear during the day and back in his rack at night. Quiet isn't bad the way we lived. Then we all heard the noise that night, metal on metal, some grinding, a squeal. You were there, Earl, looking more surprised than the rest of us, I guess because you were closer to it. That damn garbage disposal had never worked right. But that night it died, ground itself to death. I'd had a replacement waiting on Judgment Day for a long time but no money in the kitty to pay for a plumber."

"I can fix that."

"It was that guy," Casey said. "After the loud noise, his quiet voice.

"I used to be a plumber. I can fix that thing. I've done it a million times, In-Sink-Erator Pro SS. Still made in the U.S. even. Nice stainless steel grinding chamber."

"He wasn't 'that guy' anymore; he had a name, he was the Plumber now," Casey said. "I watched him poking around inside the old disposal unit, curious what took it to its death. Just as I thought the moment required a final prayer, he was set on an autopsy. He pulled out hunks of wet paper, old letters maybe, a postcard. I was angry at all you men, demanding to know who the hell was stupid enough to throw paper down the kitchen disposal? None of you had the courage to admit to it. I was mad. I pulled those little bits and scraps out, spent half the evening spreading them on the table like a jigsaw puzzle looking for clues. But most of the writing was smeared to the point where it was impossible to read. The most I got was part of a postcard, one of those ten-for-a-dollar kind tourists buy in Times Square."

"After that the Plumber did odd jobs around the area, getting some work before he moved on. I did not see him again. Good man though, smart enough not to throw away an old postcard that read GREETINGS FROM NEW YORK with half a signature saying 'Ang' or something."

Seeing the Devil

JUST CASEY AND me on the bus, plus that creepy ass Korean kid I call Tom. Getting a little darker outside, a little colder too. Still kind of pretty, that last bit of orangey-pink time of day. Even dusty windows have a purpose I guess, making sunsets look better.

"You still running the shelter Casey?"

"Have to. I've got more and more people coming in. I hear it nearly every day, 'We used to donate to you.' Now they're asking for help. The worst thing to do is nothing, so I do what I can."

"How you mean, Casey?"

"See, the thing is, I'm beginning to think we're distracted. The big issues in every election now are gay marriage, guns and abortion. Now I'm not sayin' rights aren't important, they are, but most politicians seem to just be saying things about those issues to stir up a crowd, and alienate one group from another. It's almost as if they want us to be preoccupied with some things that don't affect their profit margins to the exclusion of others that do, like the ancient Roman bread and circuses."

"Mention a word about raising the minimum wage to a living wage and either no one seems to care, or worse, you'll be blasted by pols and business owners on all sides of the other issues calling workers lazy, like they are undeserving, when they are the casualties of a war."

"We need to think about the society we live in. Inequality undermines people's faith, in government, in the economy, in each other. You start thinking justice comes only to those that can buy it. When you realize the system isn't fair, ain't meant to be fair, that the company owes you nothing, then you begin to owe them nothing, the cruelty of ambivalence. CEOs get bonuses because profits go up, whether they helped that to happen or not. Workers lose their jobs when profits go down, whether they caused that or not. Nobody caring about nothing is where it ends, or ends up. Without something to hold us together, things can't work for long. No one ever washed a rental car."

"But how do you know who to trust, Casey? My dad trusted the factory. I wanted to trust my dad, my coaches, and every one of 'em left me."

"Dammit Earl, it isn't about trust. Trust is a magic fairy dust way to try and easily resolve a really hard problem. Instead of asking you to trust me or trust each other, I want you to see what you have in common, what you share, and then have you build and organize around that. You know you all want a job, want a home, want that self-respect. You share that, and that's enough for you to work together. It may not work at first, but that's a piss-poor reason not to try. Not so many people need us anymore, but we need us."

"More than that, I'm thinking I may not be alone in this. I understand now the difference between wanting something to end and working to end it. I've been reading about these Occupy people. Reeve is a bit far off the path for anything like that, but I met a union guy in the Bullseye parking lot. He'd been beaten up pretty bad by some men who hung around looking for day work, but as soon as he's healed, he's heading back out. Maybe you know now why he stands there in the rain. There are so many of us, and it favors the few at the very top to keep us apart. Workers starving quietly isn't news, so we need to make some noise, and we make more noise when we speak together. People ask me about politics, but I really don't pay much attention. It ain't about left or right anymore, it's about up and down. Where did the 99 percent come from? We were always here, in Reeve, Ohio."

"So if you see a group standing up for themselves, look for me, because I'll be there. If you see a cop beating a man, or a kid crying because she's hungry, I'll be there. It was another preacher who said 'our lives begin to end the day we become silent about things that matter.' That isn't going to be me. I'll be there."

Casey paused, almost out of breath. It was dark outside now, even the day itself seeming to want to rest. I could see Casey was getting up to leave. All the negatives, all the cussing and contradictions, simply made Casey less of a saint, and more of a flawed human being tryin' to find a way out of a mess he'd only recently been able to even see. I knew I'd miss him then forever.

194

Casey looked out the window, then turned eye to eye with me. Serious now.

"So what'll you need, Earl?

"For what?"

"To move on, to get off this bus?"

"Casey, you was always the one with the answers. Jesus, you tell me."

"Not my place to tell, Earl. Like God needs the Devil, you gotta wrestle it yourself. Time for you to go back to work, little brother."

THE BUS STOPPED, harder this time, the brakes metal on metal like that old trash disposal back at the shelter I'd messed up with that post card.

First on was my mom.

Right behind her, my old man climbed up, still wearing his work clothes. I think he just slept in them, even now that he was dead. I never knew a man who had so many pairs of pants all the same, so many work shirts, all the same, like some Rain Man who can't stop doing the same thing over and over. I didn't smell alcohol on him, and his eyes were clear. He looked at me, meeting my own eyes for the first time since, hell, I don't know, maybe when I was a lamb in the third grade Christmas pageant and my mom made him dress up with that stupid clip-on tie. Who my dad was wasn't my choice. Not loving him was. And so if his story now was gonna be a confession, so is mine.

It was getting late on the bus. Who the hell knows how or why he was on it. I was not interested in what I expected was gonna be a "best days behind us, best days still in front of us" talk from a dead man, when all I wanted to do is get this day over with and get off this damn bus.

I was stronger than my dad when he passed, the weight almost magically transferred from him to me as he aged over the years. A part of me still wanted him to put his arms around me, hoping I could feel his strength, but I held back, knowing it was gone and not needing another reminder of that. I only saw that strength when I was younger, and then only in his anger and bitterness and the mean kind of sadness he got all over him when drinking. I remembered me and Mom would start playing a board game, and then Dad came home from work and we somehow had to stop. Or when he promised to help work on a school project, then ended up asleep on the couch instead. When your old man's dying, those are the things you want to talk about, but we was quiet.

Christ did time pass. I remember how near the end he got to climbing out of the car like it was a space capsule, the biggest part of the day was sorting out his pills for the week. Even after he died, frail, pathetic, comic, gimpy after a third stroke, I had no interest in the tears that didn't come anyway. Medicine kept him alive, but my old man died old in the strictest sense of that word.

Mom made me go through his clothes and things, saying maybe there was something I could use, and I followed her request out of habit more than respect. I wanted him to leave me something, give me stories to carry home—but there was nothing. I thought hard thoughts that day. I was alone in their bedroom, maybe for the first time in my life. I remembered being there with my friends when I was nine years old, delicately handling grandpa's gold watch. With Dad passed, I handled his things with contempt, but worried at the same time that as much as I cursed the image in the old glossy photos, I could not deny the reflection.

My mom started talking first. Every time she said my name now it sounded like she was crying:

"Earl, sweetheart, you know your Dad and me tried for you. Life turned hard. We tried not to complain about it. We didn't know what to tell you, so we said what we'd been told, to study hard, work hard, try hard—we knew hard. Your daddy loved you Earl, he wanted to see you grow up right, he thought the world of you, but we thought you wouldn't understand, maybe until you was older, so—"

"Why didn't you tell me when I got older what was inside Dad?"

"Well, your dad and me, we thought what happened, was happening, was for us to deal with, that you was always our child. What happens to adults shouldn't happen to their children, children's lives ought to be better than their parents', that was the way of it, we felt."

Mom never talked to me about her life with Dad before I was born, but it seemed now was the time to do so.

"We was married before he went to Korea. They didn't do all that with yellow ribbons back then, calling everyone heroes, and that was probably better. We had no cell phones or email, so we only knew about when he'd be back. Your grandma was the first outside when the car pulled up. Me and grandpa stayed in, him never stirring from the couch, like he knew what was coming and did not care to see it. Your dad had on his uniform, tie, shined shoes. I thought he looked wonderful."

"That night I helped him off with his undershirt, got the dog tags caught up in it. I stared at him, as it was almost shocking to see him bare-chested in front of me. Times were different then, and even though we'd been married I had not seen him in the light so naked, so close to me, much before. You're a man now, but it is still embarrassing to tell you these things, tell you I felt, well, scared and, I don't know, sexual. My night gown was like a puddle on the floor. I wanted him to put his arms around me so I could fall heavy into him, hoping I could feel his strength. How I felt like with your dad, I could never find good words for it, so I'll say it plain—I just felt. You know I never really studied much, but it was like those poems we had in Mrs. Garrity's English class, a bunch of pretty words that came one line then the next, so that at the end you didn't know why exactly, but you felt different."

"I don't know what your dad was thinking then, but his face was looking at the wall through me. He said he was just tired. I told him to come and look at the stars with me on the porch, but he said he'd already seen them. I never knew people could be tired that long that much. It felt like most of the inside of him had been left over there, leaving just the outside still with me."

"I touched him, on his chest, but he just stood there until I didn't. Put the light off and went to sleep, unrelieved from what it was. But he had that factory job waiting, it was gonna be okay, he said, soon as he could get back to work, have a schedule, have a reason for getting up early. Back then they'd save your job for you when you joined the service. Most nights he'd sleep like I had to check if he was even still breathing, then other times he'd say whispers in his sleep and toss and turn so that he'd have to untangle the sheets to get out of bed. You don't have to go over there, he said, just look into my eyes and you'll be there. I'd cry alone too many times nights. It frightened me, and so I got the courage to ask grandma about it, since grandpa had come home from his war, and she sat me down in a way that I hadn't seen since I was fourteen and learned what my period was. She said your dad just needed sleep and a drink, like grandpa had, but watch that it don't turn into too much sleep and too much drink."

ON THE BUS, I felt Dad start to talk even before he formed the words.

"Dammit, enough Sissy. I'll talk to the boy. Time's short. Jesus, there was always supposed to be more time. You, Driver, don't stop this goddamn bus 'til I'm done talking."

I hadn't heard his voice for a long time. Dad said:

They loaded us all, maybe twenty boys the Sergeant kept on calling men, on an old bus at Inchon so as to get more ass into the fight fast. We didn't know if Inchon was a town, the name of the water we saw, or some kind of Korean word for the coldest place we had ever been. We were so scared. It wasn't like we was scared of something, a roller coaster or running into an old house, just scared all the way through. People was yelling to hurry up and get into the bus, which we was doing as fast as we could on the thought that the inside of anything had to be warmer.

Inside wasn't warmer, but no one was yelling there, and we all squeezed together on the wooden seats. That wood was just like the bench on the Reeve football field sideline that had gone gray from sun. The bus pulled away and became all the world for us. They had covered the windows to make us less of a target, just slivers of sharp cold light cutting in around that edge. As the bus turned, the light would catch in the clouds of our breath in the air. Might've been pretty.

I didn't know much but I knew I was in Korea, a country that had mattered very little to Reeve, Ohio until a war started that we was told did matter. We was told that somehow North Korea the country threatened our country, as if a North Korean mountain was going to take over an Ohio field.

We had the draft then, so whether you volunteered and went this year or got drafted next year didn't matter much, and we gave the decision about as much thought as that. Being in the service was something kids from Reeve did, maybe still now like your dumb ass friend Muley. You either left high school and volunteered, or you left high school, worked a year or two in the factory, and then got drafted. Either door, you ended up in the same place as the meat cutter's kid and the school teacher's kid and the car dealer's kid and the preacher's kid. Somebody else was always rolling the dice for us.

We knew nothing about being in a war, though every one of us had played soldier for days and days in the woods and had had their turn with a rifle while chugging whiskey with our dads in a drinking contest they called 'hunting deer.' It had been poor preparation, because here there were no woods we could run through and there damn sure was no whiskey.

My dad—your grandpa—had been in the Army but he never told me much except that he walked from France to Germany in the spring of 1945 and never would care again to sleep outside or visit Europe because of it. He said he did killin' and saw killin', he said no one comes back even if their body comes back—something stays out of it. Grandpa said the best thing and worst thing was that he was ignored when he came home. He told me people would not care about what happened, they'd be on with their own lives, and if they did ask to hear, it'd only be as a cheap thrill for them. So, fuck 'em, he'd say. He said that he'd seen things he wouldn't think of but remembered anyway, remembered them like a smell or an odd sound, couldn't place it, but there it was in yer head, and the more time that passed the more he remembered. It was supposed to be the Good War, but Grandpa said it wasn't. He was supposed to be part of the Greatest Generation, but Grandpa said he wasn't. He said people who stayed home always said things like that for every war.

That was about as much detail as we'd get and even that was only after a lot of guinea red wine on Sundays, and then he'd get all quiet or yell at your grandma about something she didn't do. Grandma understood she needed to just take it, sometimes even a black eye, though he never meant no real harm, because her job was to keep Grandpa from breaking, as he was never gonna drink what bothered him off his mind. She couldn't work back then and so he had to. He walked with some limp, but we never knew why, and it never stopped him from working twelve hour shifts when he needed to. He did one time have a bit more than usual even for him at Cousin Mike's wedding and started in about piss and brains and pink shit on the snow until me and your uncle eased him outside. After that he just sat with the wine, and you kids would always laugh and say how Grandpa's sleeping at the table again.

You joined up back then and then you came home and went back to work without bellyaching. If you wanted to talk, you went to the VFW hall out on Harrisburg Road, or AmVets, though they favored the Catholics, and sat at the bar in the afternoon hiding from the sun and kicking back shots until you didn't want to talk. Some days all the wars would be there, some old bastard from the World War, another from my war, a long-hair handlestache from Vietnam, but inside we was all the same. Half the days the oldest bastard would dribble-piss himself right at the bar, until somebody saw the leak and told him, "Old man, go to the fucking toilet 'cause you forgot again."

IN KOREA ALL them years ago, the bus stopped. We all got thrown against each other, no warning, nothing we could have done.

We had not spoken. We did not know each other. We were pushed onto the buses in groups based on the order we came off the ship. Not one of these boys had struggled like me with crazy old Mrs. Reardon in 12th grade English, or done what their daddy had done in the same factory as had made me. I was certain every one of them was from somewhere else.

The Sergeant screamed at us to get off the bus. We did; there was nothing else we could have done. Outside, it was so bright, it was like comin' out of a matinée. The Sergeant pushed and cursed us into lines, his foul language a force to cause boys to shift places. He was an ugly man, the kind you look at, then look away, and then want to look back at, even knowing it's wrong to do so. It was cold and no amount of cursing was doing anything about that as we formed lines. The snow was deep enough, but we managed to pound it to hell forming up, making a little oval of flat space that was for now our home in Korea.

We had been told on the boat coming over by a chaplain that we was coming to Korea to bring the word of God to the South Koreans, kill the North Koreans, and to avoid fornication and sin. This now changed. We were luckier than a dog with two dicks, Sergeant said, because we had now a mission. The hill ahead of us, he explained while spitting into the white snow, was what we had come to Korea for. We were near a place he called Goddamn Myungdong, and we were to climb that hill, dig holes in the frozen ground and stay there until someone defeated the North Koreans. Was that clear? It was. The hill did not have a name but the Sergeant told us it was to be known as Hill 124, based on its height above sea level and thus designation on the army maps that only the Sergeant had seen or would see. Years later, as I learned more about things, it occurred to me that it was possible for other hills to be this height above sea level, and indeed several I could see around me did not look so different. It was possible that other boys would be sitting on a Hill 124 of their own, but this one was ours.

Sergeant told us we'd have time to kill when we got home after the war, now we had to work hard. We really didn't need the encouragement. The chance to do something—cut trees, slam small shovels against frozen ground—was good movement, which made us warmer and allowed us to talk to each other about this very significant hill we suddenly had in common. My small frozen hole would be near to another one with a boy whose name was Miles, a name not common in Reeve and so of some interest. We had our holes, we made our fires and, using the stomped snow as a guide, looked the other way hoping to see the North Koreans or whoever the hell might also be interested in Hill 124.

Each night felt like four weeks at Fort Polk, Louisiana, where I was basically trained, being made to eat and sleep and shit close to other men. It was there for the very first time I spoke with both a Southerner and a Negro, and on the same day ate a thing called grits. You know we're not necessarily racist in Reeve—we have Negroes living there and possibly Southerners, I don't know, but we did not readily mix. It was not something we were proud of, or not proud of, or offended by, or even gave much thought to, as we were born that way. We never had enough of the Coloreds in Reeve to become too prejudiced. Fact is, before we later all got told we was white, a lot of people in town hated men named Stephanowski, Battaglini or Abramowitz.

After many nights of absolute terror over absolutely nothing happening, we all experienced one of the most intense emotions of war—boredom. After the first night when nobody came to kill us, followed by a second, third and eighth night where nobody came to kill us, we all began to believe that on subsequent days and nights it was likely no one would come to kill us. This feeling was hastened by the reality that it appeared no one existed outside of Hill 124. We had no contact with any Koreans, except to occasionally see old women, sometimes with kids in tow, wander around in the woods, pushing aside the snow to dig around for something we came to learn was a kind of mushroom they ate. Food was scarce in Korea for the natives, but we had quite a bit of it, even though it was in the form of C-rat cans of Spam and some goop we called in a sing-song fashion, "Fruit, Peach, Canned, Syrup-Type." The Korean women and their kids would wear tin cans salvaged from us around their necks, clanging and clinking to warn us they was coming. They wanted those damn mushrooms and did not want us to shoot them, which seemed reasonable. We all waved at 'em at first, and Miles one time shouted something that meant "hello," to him at least, in Korean talk, but they'd never look at us or call back. Clang clang, dig up some mushrooms from under the damn snow, and clink clink away. Except for "hello" in Korean, which Miles claimed as his own, none of us spoke nothing but English anyway.

Even the Sergeant seemed to lighten up a bit after boredom became our general state of affairs. He may have had a name, in fact had one stenciled on his clothes like all of us, but no one here was his mother and no one would call him anything but Sergeant. Sergeant had been an occupier of Japan before bringing his skills at yelling at people to the fight in Korea. He would tell us long tales of that time in Japan, most of which revolved around having sex in exchange for food, sex for money, sex for safe passage, and then more sex. It was kind of shocking to hear it said like that. Even though we all talked about screwin', it was always kind of like we was talking about someone else, like describing a movie we'd seen, keeping a certain distance.

What appetites we had we generally kept hidden away. Sergeant was crude, saying Oriental don't matter because they all looked the same upside-down. They're little dolls over there, he'd say, can't tell the boys from the girls even turned sideways, but they'd take you away for not much money or even in exchange for a C-rat can. Had a mom, then her daughter, sayin' anyone would do anything if they was hungry enough. Paid money to some local kid who pimped out his sister in return. For an extra dollar the kid'd make her say, "I love you" in slurred English. Kissed her one time and tasted soured milk, Sergeant said with a smile. That was his element, and he fit like a fish at a swimming lesson. He said they even had fun trapped on base. One time they shoved this female dog in heat inside a cage, let her moan until every stray mutt in Japan was clawing to get in, then they opened the cage and drank beer and laughed while them dogs just about tore her apart. Said them males were so crazy they even started humping each other until someone just hit the bitch with a shovel and ended it. Can't have fun like that back home, Sergeant said.

The snow tended to absorb the sound, especially the sounds that weren't made by metal clanking against metal, so loud noises were kind of unusual, even, Miles said once, unheard of, and everybody laughed, includin' me, though I didn't quite understand everything Miles said that made people laugh. At first I thought maybe some of what he said was aimed wrong at me, but eventually we became something of friends. Anyway, one day started with a SPLAT, then another until I ended up at the bottom of my frozen hole, face pressed as hard against the frozen mud at the bottom as I could, hoping if I pushed harder then I could get deeper away from whatever this new thing was. It wasn't until I looked up finally, saw Miles standing over me and then felt the SPLAT of a well-thrown snowball hit me square in the mouth.

I climbed out of the hole to see almost every one of them soldier boys running in circles, throwing snowballs at each other and shouting, laughing and throwing more snowballs. Boredom and young boys don't mix well, and after what seemed like forever sitting on Hill 124 doing nothing, we had found something. I packed a tight one, pulling off my gloves so as to let my hands melt the snow enough to form an ice ball. With some element of a practiced eye, I hurled that snowball as hard as I could at some boy about twenty yards away, smacking him straight on his nose. He looked over at me more surprised than anything and when I saw him laugh, I laughed too and went over to make sure there were no hard feelings. His nose was bloodied all right, as I had something of an arm back then from playing football, with the red blood dripping on that white snow. As he laughed, his head moved, flinging drops of blood in a wider circle around us both. It was kinda pretty, the red and the white, the drops giving off a bit of steam and melting just a tiny bit into the crust of the snow. We shook hands and laughed, him saying he was from Indiana, which was next to Ohio and enough to form a bond of sorts that day on Hill 124.

"How old are you anyway?" I asked him. "Eighteen. Next month," he said.

I never felt old before. I had just myself turned nineteen.

I looked over and Miles had a bunch of boys making snow angels in formation, flopping down in the snow and waving their arms around, swinging their legs open and shut, then hopping up just as quick to make another, until most of us were lying in the snow making designs, laughing at the fun of it, happy for the first time to be on Hill 124. We saw some Koreans clinking their way toward their mushrooms and waved, some of us even getting up long enough to throw a snowball at the kids towed along behind their mamas.

It will be no surprise that the Sergeant's voice cut through it all. Sergeant began running up the hill, kicking boys still half buried in snow, grabbing their arms and pulling them back to their holes, yelling at us for being idiots out in the open and that we had a job to goddamn do.

There is nothing in the world that sounds like a mortar. No time to be brave or scared at first. Later, when you have time to sort it out, you recall a distant, hollow thunk, then a whistle, then an explosion. Them three sounds come one-by-one but feel when they happen like one big thing, but they are distinct. The thunk comes as the shell ignites in the mortar tube somewhere far away, the whistle as that shell moves from there to you, and then the explosion. You feel that thunk in your chest as much as you hear it, and it stays with you so as to make you jump twenty years later when something hollow hits the floor behind you, or when your goddamn son stomps up the stairs, Earl. We had learned at Fort Polk that mortar shells are well-designed, simple enough to have been around for many wars, but improved in World War II to include specially cut grooves and ridges so that the explosion inside the shell turns the casing holding it all together into white-hot pieces of scientifically designed metal fragments, each blown into a razor-sharp edge. The large pink-faced Southerner who explained this to us in basic training likened it to a Tootsie Pop, as the hard candy shell was good to eat as well as the casing holding the whole Pop together.

We did not know whether it was the noise we made, the movement we made on Hill 124, or simply one of those coincidences that caused mortar shells to fall on us twenty or so boys making snow angels. Maybe some of us was marked to die a long time ago, even sitting on the bus from Inchon, and this was just when it happened, or maybe every round was To Whom It May Concern, like a car accident. We did not know if the mortar shells were fired by our men, North Korean men or spit out by an angry God, but they did fall on us and it did not matter why or what we thought about it. The snow did its job, deadening the sound of the explosions, catching some of the shrapnel, which, white-hot, made tiny puffs of steam as it melted through the frozen crust, and then absorbing the fluid of several boys, one from Indiana still suffering from a bloody nose. I was fine, not hurt, some dirt blown into my mouth and on my teeth, just watching the impressions of snow angels fill with blood around me as Hill 124 tried to kill us.

In a decent world that would have been the end of that day. I would have walked home, had dinner, maybe asked my own dad about what had happened. Going to a warm bed and waking up the next morning usually solved problems in Reeve, as many times the smell of a new day absorbed what had passed the night before. But I was not there, I was as far away from there as it was possible to be, so I heeded the Sergeant and ran to my hole. I hated him for seeming necessary then, hated Hill 124 for making men like the Sergeant necessary, and hated myself for knowing so little about the details of what was necessary now to save my own life. It was clear that whatever that Sergeant knew about whores and cursing, he did know equally about the real side of war that had just been visited on me, so I ran to my hole and, following his shouts, prepared and aimed my rifle forward expecting the North Koreans or maybe Satan himself to emerge from those woods.

Miles was also okay. After some time had passed, he shouted my name, "Ray Ray Ray, did they get you?" and I felt more alive than ever to be able to say, "No, I am here." Sergeant was telling us that the war was most certainly coming, to stay alert, to shoot as needed, to not hesitate to defend Hill 124. And I believed I should do this as strongly as anything I have ever believed.

Time passed, what might have been twenty minutes as easily as several hours. The sun was still high, the sky still that unbelievable blue. Nature had reset itself, even as we cautiously had been pulled out of our holes by the Sergeant to retrieve the bodies of the boys dead behind us. It smelled like copper. I had no sense that people had so much blood in them until I saw it all spread out. It had been red, redder than you'd think, but by then had turned darker, sorta chocolate against the snow still white. Not killed, destroyed. I only looked at one of them faces. I could see blood running like little creeks between his zit pimples.

Sergeant had us organized so that most stayed in their holes pointing their rifles into the woods while one or two were called back to help with the bodies. Sergeant said help was going to come, to start the boys home who had gotten killed and to replace them so all the holes could be refilled on Hill 124. Sergeant seemed to know what to do, and that was a powerful thing. It made us feel we could fight off whoever came at us through those woods in what he called the follow-on attack.

More time passed, and soon enough the dead were collected. By the time it was my turn to help collect them, the boys had turned stiff from the cold, making it harder to pull them into a resting position. The sudden silence as the work ceased scared us more, amplifying every sound around us. Then came evening. This would be the time, Sergeant said.

The noise that startled me first was harsh enough to make me cry out some kind of sound from deep in my stomach I had never known was in there. I stood up, foolishly, and pointed off to the right where the sound came from. Without warning Miles and several other of the boys began shooting. The last time I'd heard a military rifle fire was in Louisiana, where there was no snow, and so I almost did not recognize the sound as a friendly one here. I could hear the rounds cutting through the air, and I dropped down into my hole. My leg felt warm, unnaturally so, and I realized as it started to freeze that I had pissed myself. I was so scared I felt no shame, or should I say the fear took up so much of me that shame would have to wait its turn. The shooting stopped on its own, not quite as suddenly as it started. It became silent again on Hill 124, purposefully so, and I raised my head.

It was the Sergeant again, yelling at me and Miles to crawl out into the woods and see what had happened. This was a word I had learned in basic training called reconnoiter, but now it was not a word, but my whole being. I was to reconnoiter, and I might die doing it, simply because someone had told me that was what I was to do next. Given that on my own I had shouted like a girl and peed myself, I had few options left but to do what I was told. Getting out of that hole was how I was going to redeem myself from the failure to act like a man when the moment first called me.

Miles and I crawled forward, not feeling the cold nor smelling the lingering coppery blood smell that would have at any other time overwhelmed us. It seemed in such conditions your brain and your senses reorganized so that some things mattered more than others. I was grateful for the snow, hiding the frozen black stain on my right leg.

We heard another sound, ahead, and came up on our knees behind the birch trees to see further. Both of us raised our rifles, aiming carefully at absolutely nothing, playing soldier, the stances and actions we had seen in the movies overpowering the scant basic training in proper technique. The sound that came from our side as we were aiming the wrong way was a SPLAT, then another, followed by cold snow down the back of my jacket, the collar hunched open as I squinted down my rifle's length. We shouted and ran, grabbing the goddamn Korean kid who had thrown snowballs at us, drawn forward and separated from his mother once the mortar shells flew in from Hell, throwing snowballs because he had seen us doing it, smiling stupidly, a way to reach us without speaking our language, wanting us to join with him somehow. I was angry, I hated that child for almost drawing me into killing him that day on Hill 124.

While Miles ran back to tell the Sergeant, I grabbed the kid, who was maybe young enough not to have been scared by the mortars, or maybe old enough to know what mortars were and how the fate that guides them in means it isn't worth being frightened over. I grabbed him and slapped and punched him. Tears ran, and I kept hitting that bastard child, wanting to say I hated what had happened, hated what I had almost done, hated myself for peeing on myself, hated that snow and hated Hill 124.

I dragged that child back to the Sergeant, knowing the Sergeant would know what I should do next. I was done. I was dead standing there, and the Sergeant could kick me or curse me as he wished. Instead, I heard him say I had done a good thing bringing the little bastard in, that maybe the North Koreans were using the kid to locate us, to direct their mortars, to draw us out, to report back. These people were animals, would do anything if they got hungry enough. Kind words of praise from a man who usually had none, and they warmed me. Sergeant said he would interrogate the child, find out what was what and that I should return to my hole. I was then glad to do so.

It had become a heavy dark with no moon. I allowed myself to believe there would be no follow-on attack, that the mortars had likely been fired accidentally by our own men, just as scared as I was, that the kid in the woods was just a kid separated from his mother, that she hadn't been killed by a stray mortar round to separate them, that the Sergeant would no more learn any secret intelligence from that kid than I would be able to stop smelling my own urine on myself, though it was long frozen stiff. I wondered if it got easier. I wondered if it got better. Because right then, I was just so tired. Silent but for the lifting sounds of someone hurting, which I quickly realized had been coming from the Sergeant's hole. He had taken seriously the task of trying to get the child to talk, though God only knows what and why and how they could even communicate. None of that had come into my head when the Sergeant had praised me for bringing that boy in from the woods, and when he seemed so sure of what to do to protect us, what we—he—had to do for Hill 124.

People who have never been in the service, or prison I guess, undervalue simple things like being free to walk away from something. You, Earl, talk all the time about good and evil, Heaven and Hell, but you don't know anything about those things. I knew—I knew that this was not a place where men changed for the better. Instead, men with flaws turn bad, and bad men come to evil. I walked over to the Sergeant and I saw him bent over that child in the bloody snow at the bottom of the hole, the kid's hard almond eyes not blinking.

"Go away goddammit Ray, and don't say nothing," hissed that Sergeant. "This ain't your business." And he turned back on the child with his fists, knowing as sure as I had pissed myself earlier that I would turn away and never say nothing. I never did, until now I guess. That was it. They didn't do investigations back then, and they didn't have no shrinks. Whatever happened just happened, and you were supposed to get over it.

But nothing about me was ever the same. It was, I came to think, like taking one of those jigsaw puzzles apart piece by piece. You couldn't say exactly when, but at some point you couldn't see the picture anymore. I ain't going to be saved from this, and I know in my heart God is not the only one justified to make such calls. I ain't saying this absolves me of all the good I failed to do, for Mom and you, but I wanted you to know, now, finally, that there was more to me than just drink and laziness.

I went to church most Sundays 'cause your mother bitched at me if I didn't, but I never believed in God again. You take care of your mother wherever she ends up, Earl. Me, I'll listen for you knocking on Hell's door, because I was the Devil that day on Hill 124.

End of the Line

ONE MORE STOP before the end of the line, the Driver called out. Night, dark as Hell. I was alone on the bus, now, finally, even the creepy Korean kid was done with me. To say I survived is not the same as to say I'm alive, because I woke up to find that my dad's wars, not just in Korea, but Ohio, too, survived with me.

I'd been squatting in a trailer, abandoned or maybe more truthfully, given up, by some earlier failure. Trailer parks were purgatory, where you sorted out if you were gonna get up and afford an apartment, or slide back down. Those parks were lonely places during the day, with just enough people around to make them seem more deserted than they were. Parents at work or looking, kids at school or running away somewhere, playing on the swings in the park, back and away, back and away. If you didn't live retired in one of God's waiting rooms down in Florida, it was an adjustment to being around mostly people younger than you. I never had any kids, so I only saw it all once.

With kids you kinda get a second look at life, and I lost out on that too. Age is the only disease you don't want to get cured from. Nights, Angie, dammit, Angie danced through my dreams, as an adult now, giving me memories of things that never happened. Remembering is a curse when there was no space in a shittin' room for anything bigger than memories. I had just one light in the place, and I was like a shadow running from it.

I was so cold. I should've worn a coat before I shot myself, but after three days and nights staying awake afraid of what I'd be dreaming, I was thinking only about the comfort of that Glock 9 mm and not about a coat. My mom's voice was always there in my head, even before I started seeing her on this bus, so I was wearing decent underwear as a matter of habit. Some things, right? It was just after lunch, but I already was worried it'd be goodbye to my sleep for the night again too. I was thinking I should feel tired, like I did in the late afternoons, but instead I just thought about the gun. I felt the bullet's speed, felt it inside me, felt it pinch me to death. Others would think about the pain, but I just thought about the sleep. Maybe in another time, another place, I could have taken something, one of those medicines they advertise on TV to ask my doctor about, to help me blend in to it all, but here it seemed better to just get out. There was a fine line between having to think of reasons to pick yourself up off the floor and picking up that gun.

The days were syrup. My fading breath on the cold window. One table, one chair, one spoon, one fork. My day, lacking an alternative, started. 7:46. I made up little routines, opening the blinds in the morning, adjusting them throughout the afternoon as if that was a job in itself. 9:37. The sun was strongest this time

217

of year just about when SpongeBob came on, so I closed the blinds then. 10:42. What did I actually need to do in a day that actually mattered? I wrote "clip nails" on a to-do list so there'd be something there, then crossed it off when I finished. 2:17. There's a human need to feel some purpose, some point in bothering to get off the floor in the morning. I took to studying the TV schedule, starting to anticipate certain shows, thinking obscenely too much about what'll happen in a drama that stood in for real life. 3:10. I wish I believed enough to pray. 3:12. Why not just give it up and watch TV and drink some more? I memorized the noises of my trailer, the pacing of the refrigerator, the hum of some electrical motor. Somebody laughing outside, maybe a woman crying next door? Music from another trailer, songs from another place. I so wanted all those things on TV—they'd double my order if I called now—not outta desire but just to, I don't know, participate. There was so much to want. 5:15. Without anything really purposeful, I became obsessed with so little, a hostage with nothing but too much time. Light slurring to shadow across my afternoon. Some days I couldn't hear my own voice, and didn't want to.

Ain't nowhere lonelier than a liquor store. You go in at ten in the morning and feel like you gotta explain why you're there at ten in the morning, forgetting that they open that early 'cause they know exactly why you're there. Roll in at eight on a Saturday night and there's seven guys staring shoulder to shoulder at rows of bottles saying nothing to each other. Maybe some young kid'll rush in on the way to a party to buy margarita mix or something as a sign that life goes on, but that's about the only sign you have a right to expect. I started drinking more and more Everclear, 99 percent pure alcohol, all octane, just made to get you drunk with no taste or flavor added, because they knew you didn't care anymore. Another perfect product for a new market, and the state collected tax on it, so everyone wins. The stuff tastes like drinking hand sanitizer, 'cept on those days when you didn't care if you were drinking hand sanitizer, and then those jolts tasted like Heaven. God bless.

Drinking helped but hurt. It was something more to look forward to, the first fizzy beer of the day tickling inside my nose or the throat-burning shot of something stronger biting into my ulcer. Drinking wiped away hours, when I felt I had too many of them. So many that I wanted to throw some away, then one day just fucking throw them all away, the old ones and the future ones—all of them.

6:05. Sweet Jesus, the alcohol. It was always the things I did to cope that got me. There'd be the soft, blurry part where the alcohol swarmed my brain, happily swerving me away from an even line, but sooner and sooner those good feelings would lose out to just feeling empty again, falling into my past, so it was fool's gold. My eyes were screwed on to the end of long tunnels, and my stomach shouted with the burn. More drinking chased those feelings away for shorter and shorter spans until the rhythms got so close they disappeared and, I just felt too much, which was the same to me as feeling nothing. 10:25. I had little control over what happened to me and my life. So, I decided then that I would decide when I was gonna die, not letting God do it. It was dead lonely until that click and the BANG, more surrender for me than an act of will.

∾   ∾   ∾

SO NOW YOU know it. I lied. It wasn't no accident when I shot myself.

SHOOTING MYSELF HURT a lot less than I expected, not that hurt should be a prime consideration when dead is the goal. People always say, "I hope he didn't suffer," forgetting about them fifty-two early warning signs. I had had the gun for a while, owning it for no particular reason along with a badminton set I am pretty sure I used as often as the gun. It held seventeen bullets, of which I only needed the one, leaving the other sixteen as useful and needed as that badminton set. I bought the Glock at a pawn shop, same place I once pawned my old man's dad's gold watch for booze money after he died. I went back when I had a little green, looking to see if the watch was still there—you know, just curious—and ended up with the gun instead. A CLICK before the BANG. The Glock company is foreign, and only does some assembly in the U.S. so they can qualify for government contracts. Still, people call it "America's Favorite Handgun."

I realized I had gone four days—or was it five?—without talking to another person. Without a job and money, you are slowly erased from other peoples' lives. I stopped remembering when I was stronger, playing ball and swimming, and saw myself turned into something I never thought I'd become. Those good memories became scabs I picked at, and for the picking they'd just grow back crustier. My inside had atrophied as much as my muscles, giving up being a sort of shameful, sort of peaceful secret I kept with myself. I'm not sure when I changed from being unbreakable to being a late fall leaf, but it happened. Now

I'm just a big sour bag of skin full of gin, self-pity and resentment crawling into another pale coma after a night of drinking, allergic to life, exempt from grace. I didn't get old, I just ran out of future. People talk about how sad it is to hit your peak early, like the best years of your life were behind you on some high school football field. Fair enough, but what if you never had any best years? What if all you had was a steady hum that just sorta ended? It wasn't more than fifty-two years of swimming against a tide I had only recently come to see—never mind understand—that brought me back to that pawn shop that day. I walked in thinking about my old man's dad's gold watch I had pawned what must have been fifteen years ago, thinking it should still be on the shelf, magically, simply because now I wanted to see it again and believing fate owed me one—and I walked out with the Glock 9 mm instead, setting me up for the trip to this bus as sure as one step leading to another. Another guy would've bought a twelve gauge and a bag of fresh shells to take into the place he just got fired from, but that wasn't me. I bought that Glock on time payments, and only made the one before using her today, so much for that business decision. And they say as long as you keep your sense of humor, you'll be okay.

The Driver slid the bus to the curb. Last stop.

I looked out the window, wiping the condensation away with my hand. There was a woman out there at the bus stop.

Kim?

No, at first I thought it was Kim from the strip mall, or maybe even Jodie from Bullseye, but it wasn't either of them, probably couldn't have been.

I watched Angie climb on to the bus.

"Hey Earl."

I'd been holding it in a long time, rain building up in the clouds like a summer storm.

"Angel. I missed you. I screwed up leaving you. You were worth every breath, everything. I'm so sorry—"

"Easy Earl, easy, friend. Nothing to be sorry about."

"Angie, you knew, didn't you, about Reeve, about the factory, our life?"

"Naw, I didn't know much except that Reeve was an old story and I wanted a new one. Things went okay enough for me, but I'm just one person. Around me, too many people on my bus still weren't okay, and it pulled at me the same as at you. Our folks were better people than they became."

"I should have gone with you that day."

"Maybe—it would've been fun to have you along for the ride, Earl. But you're asking the wrong question."

"What?"

"It ain't so much why you didn't come with me that one day, it's more why you didn't leave Reeve every day after that."

"You were gone, Angie, I didn't know where to find you, and—"

"Earl, that road was always there."

What Angie was for me, hell, she was so many things. But as she sat there it was like someone finally turned up the volume on the radio so I could hear it. I knew then that what she really was there for was to tell me I had to choose between the old story, my dad's life in Reeve, and the possibility of more than that. To me, then, I hadn't even seen the choice, only the false comfort of the familiar, the jobs will come back, manufacturing will be reborn under the new president, or with green initiatives or high-tech or fairy dust sprinkles. I didn't have the guts to not follow in my father's footsteps, even as I hated him, and I hated me, for doing it, and I ended up following the same bad spiral that took the country down. Like many people in American towns such as Reeve, I existed in a world that only got smaller. I couldn't think beyond it.

The idea that somehow at the end I could change pain into beauty, it wasn't any more true than the movies, at least it wasn't for me. No whores with hearts of gold, no self-taught janitors with noble ambitions, no meek inheriting anything. Just a helluva lot of damaged people, some still trying out of habit—our inherent stubbornness—and some done. Me, I was done.

THERE WAS A long pause. The Driver stopped. It was quiet on the bus.

"Hey Earl, you remember once in the park, on the swings? What was it you kept saying while you pushed me?"

"I said, back and a-wwway, Angie, back and a-wwwway."

"That was what your mama said to you, wasn't it, when you were little?"

"Yeah, my dad too, sometimes, I guess."

"Earl, you gotta know now, I gotta tell you, a few months after I left Reeve with you, you know, when you turned back, I had a baby. I must've been pregnant when I left that day."

"Me?"

"Maybe, probably . . . of course, yeah, he *is* you Earl. Looks like you, talks like you, sometimes sad, sometimes kinda funny, summer birthday and brown eyes, a good kid like you. I didn't tell you, well, you never called me, and I even sent you that one postcard. It was hard, me being just a kid too, but we got by."

"Angie—"

"You left something here Earl, world knows you were here. That boy's now—"

"A boy?"

"He's a man now, Earl, but you have a son out there that's just getting started on his bus ride. Gonna do something with himself, wants to help people."

"Angie, if he wants to help people, you tell him about the hash I made of my life. Tell him he can have a society where the majority of people flounder just above poverty, the water risen right up to their literal New Orleans lips. Or, he can choose a society where people have more hope. His group—and there are 99 of him to every one of them—have to stop buying the old story. Most people understand the boss takes more, they just want enough. Farmers pray for rain, not a different system of weather. Rain works. Tell him he don't need socialism or wealth redistribution or handouts or a hand up or bailouts or welfare or food stamps or safety nets, just work where he can find his self-worth, create a reality that he can—I could have—well, lived with. You tell him that."

"Okay now, it's almost done. Shhh, no more talking Earl."

"Can I hold you?

"'Course. But time is short."

"I never knew my arms could be a bad place for you to be. I wish there was more, Angie."

"Me too. You know, Earl, it doesn't really end when you do. I can see you in his face, the way he sits, what he says, his smile. When people look in his eyes, you'll be there. You're on our bus, same as we were on yours."

Angie smiled at me, and asked, as if we had always been together, when was the last time I'd had really good spaghetti, and if I still liked apples, like we hadn't not talked for all those years. She slid her hand down my arm, past the wrist, to 1977. I looked at her, seeing her sixteen, then back to myself, tanned almost chocolate to the shirt sleeves, strong again. Sixteen-year-old girls are wasted on seventeen-year-old boys. I never understood that it wasn't what we did or what we said, it was all about what we were when we were with each other. Some say it's about the bus ride—life—but at some point it just ends. The journey's all we have until we get there.

Angie took my finger in her mouth, I felt her tongue, warm and a little coarse, and she whispered to me that she wanted to curl around it until it's all inside of her. It became my last memory.

It was effortless.

The bullet I had just launched passed through my brain. What seemed like a lifetime had been just a fraction of a second, all that I remembered passing through my soul in a single moment. Things turned red, then white, then gray, as my eyes filled with night. My body was so heavy, then so light, until I was made more of air than of me, rising. At about this point the bullet completed what I had sent it to do.

I kissed Angel goodbye. It was time to get off the bus.

Acknowledgments

YOU MAY WRITE alone, but you don't think alone. Thanks to the many people who read alongside me and helped make this all better: Mari Nakamura, Lisa Ehrle, Teri Schooley, Dan White, Randy "Charlie Sherpa" Brown, Bruce Levine, Connie Lockwood, Steve, Matthew Hoh, Alex Kingsbury, David Rubenstein, Alyssa Frohberg and Tom DeLong.

Special thanks to friends Jesselyn Radack, John Kiriakou, Tom Drake, and Teresa Hartnett, to Dr. Morris Berman for the inspiration, and to Laurie Russo, a help (again) as an early editor. And thanks to Tracy Richardson, Chris Katsaropoulos, and the team at Luminis for producing a beautiful book.

About the Author

PETER VAN BUREN, a 24-year veteran of the State Department, spent a year in Iraq. Following his first book, *We Meant Well: How I Helped Lose the Battle for the Hearts and Minds of the Iraqi People*, the Department of State began proceedings against him as a whistleblower. Through the efforts of the Government Accountability Project and the ACLU, Van Buren instead retired from the State Department with his full benefits of service.

Prior to Iraq, Van Buren was assigned to Taiwan, Osaka, London, Seoul, Tokyo and other locations in East Asia. He attended The Ohio State University, graduating with a B.A. in photography and an M.A. in education. He also attended Osaka University of Foreign Studies and Hyogo University of Teacher Education for post-graduate study. His commentary has appeared in *The New York Times, Salon, Mother Jones, Huffington Post, NPR,* and on the BBC. Having grown up in Ohio, Van Buren now lives in New York City.

Learn more at www.ghostsoftomjoad.com